Flurry the Bear

The Assassin's Pact

J.S. Skye

The Assassin's Pact
(Flurry the Bear – Book 6)
Copyright © 2017 J.S. Skye
All rights reserved.
www.FlurryTheBear.com

Cover art by Luís Figueiredo, J.S. Skye, & Tony Washington

ISBN: 0998857718
ISBN-13: 978-0998857718

CONTENTS

CHAPTER 1
THE ADVENTURER

The leaves rustled as numerous footsteps trampled the vibrantly-colored, fallen beauties. Furry figures rushed through the foliage. Blades of grass and large fern leaves parted every which way as the caravan's white-furred leader weaved between the trees.

Shouts could be heard in the distance. "Flurry! Stop! Flurry! Wait for us!"

The snow-colored cub ran with all of his might out ahead of the others. He was a bear on a mission. Flurry frantically charged on through the warm-hued forest until he reached a clearing with a small settlement that sat next to a set of railway tracks up ahead. "They have to be here somewhere. They couldn't have gone far," Flurry softly spoke to himself.

In the middle of his thought, screams were heard from the settlement. "Help! Somebody, please help! They're here!" came shouts from the multitude of residents.

"Ah ha!" Flurry exclaimed and ran toward the commotion.

Boaz, Noah, Caboose, and Honja ran out of the woods, just a few paces behind their teddy bear brother. "Flurry, wait!" shouted Boaz, but he did not receive a reply.

Flurry rushed through the brick-laid streets of the tiny town. He looked to and fro. "Where are they?" he shouted at the bystanders. The fear stricken occupants of the community pointed Flurry in the correct direction.

The cub took off like a flash of lightning. He dodged farm animals and onlookers alike as he rushed after his quarry. Boaz and the other cubs desperately tried to keep up.

Boaz had a moment of relief when he and the others caught up with their brother while he stood still for an abbreviated moment to scout the alleyways. "Flurry, please stop! We're out of our league here! We need to wait for the others," came the desperate plea of the little lion cub as he adjusted his thick-framed glasses.

"No time!" Flurry shouted and darted down an alley. He leapt up onto a carriage drawn by miniature horses, to Boaz's dismay.

"What in the world are you doing?" Boaz shouted and chased after the bear cub. "That doesn't belong to you!"

"I'm just borrowing it! Okay, goodbye!" came Flurry's reply.

"Hey!" came the bellow of the owner, a middle-aged groundhog.

Boaz ran up to the fierce-looking rodent whom Flurry left in the dust. The lion cub handed him some gold coins. "I'm terribly sorry about this, sir. He'll return your horses to you, I promise! He's just borrowing them." After he received a paw full of money, the groundhog was pleased enough to concede his horses and carriage for the time being.

A loud crash caught Noah's attention. The tall, slender lion tapped on Boaz's shoulder and pointed down the street. "Oh no!" came the little lion cub's reply. Boaz looked on toward the chaos. Out ahead, he saw that Flurry had crashed into all manner of things as he sped off on the carriage. "Quickly!" Boaz shouted and ran in the direction of the mess. Noah, Caboose, and Honja followed close behind.

Boaz ran over to the vendors in the marketplace and found many of them with food knocked down and strewn all over the ground. "What a mess!" Caboose commented. "Mommy would cry if she saw sis."

Boaz groaned at Flurry's behavior, and gave money to each of the vendors to pay for the havoc that Flurry made. "I'm terribly sorry about all of this. Please forgive the mess." Boaz seemed to have his paws full as he played the role of Flurry's public relations lion.

Meanwhile, Flurry rode the miniature horses hard. The small carriage bounced with each bump, hole, and rock in the path. Flurry made a beeline for the railway that had a steam powered engine of some kind prepared for departure.

The cars were being loaded full of goods and riches stolen from the town Flurry had trashed with his commandeered carriage. In addition to the stolen goods, there were prisoners that had been tied up with ropes. These captives were also being taken aboard.

The captors were ominous in appearance. They seemed to be similar to goats with long fur under their jaw that made their heads look rectangular. Their fur was midnight blue, and they had very large horns that curled toward the back of their heads. Their eyes looked hollow and empty, as if they were without souls.

A majority of them were dressed in shiny armor with swords and spears, but their leader was different. The one in charge was named Naphal. Flurry had learned of his identity a few days prior to this sunny morning. Naphal was larger than the others of his kind, and he was hunched over as though he were elderly. His chin hair was long and woven together in a braid that hung down below his knees. He wore a hooded robe and carried a large staff instead of a weapon.

Flurry learned that nobody had a rightful name for these beasts. They were simply known as the Gatemakers, and they lived in a hidden dimension. They traveled to and from their world through a gateway only they knew how to open or close.

Their leader, Naphal, had terrorized the inhabitants of various lands for many generations. Without warning, Naphal and his fellow Gatemakers would appear and kidnap a multitude of victims to be taken back to their world for whatever dark purposes they had in store. Nobody ever returned.

Flurry swiftly approached. He quickly deduced that these Gatemakers were so numerous that he stood no chance against them. *If only I had some help*, Flurry thought to himself.

However, Flurry did not have time to think about his odds of success. He had a mission at hand, and he was not about to fail. Ever since Flurry's pirate adventure, something had changed inside of him. He no longer glorified pirates or the act of piracy, as he once had. Flurry now held to a vow he had purposed in his heart to keep. Flurry had found something new to be dedicated to, something more than himself. His new purpose was to help anyone and everyone he could. So, Flurry was quite motivated to catch up with Naphal and the Gatemakers, stop them, and save the day. In addition to that, his friend was one of the captives, and Flurry could not let anything happen to him.

Flurry hollered at the horses to press them for more speed. He leaned forward and whipped the reins harder. He was gaining on the steam engine that now coasted away from him along the tracks. He continued to near his target when a large shadow was cast across the ground and Flurry's carriage.

Suddenly, there was a loud thump on top of the carriage. Startled, Flurry spun around and looked back. He let out a sigh of relief at the sight of Chingu. The red panda stood heroically on the carriage roof. Flurry returned to guiding his carriage. Faith, his trusty reeyu, glided on past.

"You scared me!" the cub shouted back at the red panda warrior. Chingu's reply was nothing more than extending his paw to point at the getaway train. Flurry knew that he had Chingu's approval for his hasty actions, and it motivated him to push on.

Flurry neared the last car. Chingu leapt from the carriage and onto the train. The warrior stood up and pulled his elegant blade from its scabbard. A bright, shining hue of blue radiated from the metal to indicate pure evil was near. It could mean none other than the presence of Naphal. The Gatemakers prepared for battle. Chingu made his way across the train cars and cut down his enemies one-by-one. The red panda was greatly outnumbered, but he was not anywhere close to being outmatched. Chingu's skill with the blade was unparalleled by the enemies he now met head-on.

Chingu fought his way to the front of the train. There were only a few of them left. From the lead car, Naphal turned to glare at Chingu – his horns were exceptionally large to denote his authority. He showed no concern for the red panda samurai, turned his back, and continued to prepare for the opening of a dimensional gateway. A brief moment later, a black hole opened up ahead of the train. Purple light spun and swirled around its dark center.

It was now or never. Chingu knew that once they passed through the gateway, nothing would return. Chingu separated his sword and fought with a blade in each paw. Left and right, his enemies dropped by his swords.

The noble warrior approached the prisoners and cut their ropes. "Quickly! We have to get off before it's too late."

"How?" asked another red panda. This red panda was not just another prisoner, but was none other than Chingu's brother, Shinyuu.

"I don't know yet, but we have to think fast," Chingu replied.

Naphal glanced over momentarily, but was unconcerned. He turned his back and looked toward his exit which fast approached.

"Here! Over here!" came a shout. Chingu, Shinyuu, and the other prisoners looked up and saw the reeyu glide back down from above. Drizzle rode on Faith's back. She drifted close beside the train. "Jump, now!" Drizzle shouted.

Chingu looked at his brother and nodded. Shinyuu and the other prisoners jumped onto the reeyu's back.

The extra weight made the reeyu lose altitude. Before long, the reeyu fell to the ground and slid across the dirt on her belly. Everyone was flung from her back and hurtled to the ground. The runaway train sped into the glowing gateway and vanished.

It was over. The sound of horses approached. "Guys! Guys! Are you okay?"

came Flurry's inquiry as he rode up and brought the carriage to a halt.

The cub jumped down and rushed over to Drizzle's side. "Driz! Driz! Are you okay?" Flurry had given Drizzle a nickname, because he thought it was easier to say.

"Huh?" asked the black-furred bear. "Oh, hi, Flurry. Yes, I'm fine. Thank you."

"No problem, pal," Flurry replied before he rushed off to check on Chingu and Shinyuu.

Everyone seemed to be okay, prisoners and all. Shinyuu stood up and brushed the dirt off his clothes. He stood up and was taken off guard when Chingu's paw smacked him across the back of the head.

"Ouch!" Shinyuu bellowed. "What was that for?"

"Do you really have to ask?" Chingu

replied. "How many times have you been captured now? I've lost count." Shinyuu giggled nervously and blushed.

Flurry rushed over to Faith, his fallen reeyu. "Faith! Are you okay, girl?" he asked as he patted her on the head. She replied by licking Flurry on the face.

Drizzle and Chingu helped the prisoners into the carriage while Shinyuu took the driver's seat in preparation to bring everyone back to the neighboring town.

Flurry mounted the reeyu, and Drizzle rushed up and jumped on Faith's back, too. Chingu sat next to his brother on the carriage, and off they all went.

When they entered the town, the groundhog, prairie dog, and mole inhabitants of the small mining settlement rushed out to greet them. Everyone cheered.

The freed captives disembarked from the carriage and hugged their loved ones. Some of the groundhogs grabbed Flurry, lifted him up on their shoulders, and paraded him around the streets as their hero.

"Of course! He steals a carriage, wrecks the town, and then gets treated like a hero! How typical!" grunted Boaz while he and the other cubs stood by and watched.

"Sat looks fun!" Caboose chimed in.

Noah and Honja stood by and observed the merriment.

Before long a Savannah cat, dressed like the Savanis medjay of legend, came out from the forest, followed by a crowd of more freed captives. He had a decorative gold neck plate with a blue gemstone laid in its center. His head was adorned with a gray and gold striped headdress, and he wore a blue and red loin cloth with a gold hem. The heavily decorated Savannah cat led his party to the cheerful crowd gathered on the street. The prairie dogs, groundhogs, and moles all reunited with their loved ones as they kissed and hugged.

The cat approached Chingu and Shinyuu. "Well done!" said the yellow-furred feline.

"You weren't so bad yourself," Chingu replied.

"Thank you so much for your help!" exclaimed the town's leader. He smiled at Chingu and the others that stood nearby. "Without all of you, my daughter would've been lost to me forever. This won't be forgotten."

"It was nothing," Chingu replied. "It's what we do."

The town officials tried to offer money,

but Chingu refused. Boaz could not believe it, so he rushed up quickly to intervene. "Chingu's just being modest, a little for food and supplies would be appreciated," said the lion cub.

The groundhog handed Boaz some money just as Flurry approached. "Well, it looks like somebody's having a good time," came Boaz's sarcastic comment.

"Yeah, I am," Flurry replied with a giggle. Boaz huffed with frustration. Flurry grabbed the reins of the horses and led them down the street to their proper owner. "Thank you Mr. … Groundhog."

"No problem. Thank you for being such a fine, noble fellow," came the reply of the carriage owner.

Boaz threw a fit when he saw such a gracious response to whom Boaz thought of as a horse thief. "Ah! I see what this is all about," he chimed in while he trailed behind Flurry.

"What?" Flurry replied.

"I thought it was suspicious that you'd be so motivated to help everyone over the past couple of months. Now it's clear to me. This is about getting all of the attention, isn't it?"

"What?" the cub exclaimed. "Don't be silly! I just want to help others."

"Sure you do!" came the sarcastic, disbelieving reply. Flurry walked off to join Chingu and Shinyuu as Drizzle approached Boaz.

"What's going on?" asked Drizzle.

"I think Flurry's doing all of this to get attention. What do you think?" Boaz asked.

"No. I think he genuinely cares," Drizzle replied.

"What?" exclaimed the lion. "How can you say that? You, more than anyone, know what he's like."

"Yes, but you've seen how well we've gotten along over the past two months. What does he have to gain from that?"

"Yeah, you have a point … I guess."

"A friend!" Caboose replied. "Did I win? Was it suh right answer?"

Drizzle giggled. Boaz groaned. "Sure! It's good enough for me," Drizzle replied and then patted Caboose on the head.

The evening sun came quickly and was close to vanishing below the horizon. Chingu wanted to continue on their journey back to Ursus right away, but the town's inhabitants insisted they stay the night. Flurry and his friends found themselves being given nice rooms, warm meals, and comfy beds for the night.

Flurry and the rest of his friends sat on the floor to play a game, Shinyuu napped, the Savannah cat stood watch, and Chingu sharpened his sword while he conversed with Honja privately.

Honja typically kept to himself, but Chingu spoke the same language as Honja. After a considerable amount of time on the road, since the day that Flurry and the others found themselves floating at sea, Honja warmed up to the red panda.

However, things were not so cozy between Honja and Boaz. The two used to be the closest of friends. It seemed that nothing would ever stand between them, until a couple of weeks ago.

Boaz was now giving Honja the silent treatment. He felt justified in cutting Honja out of his life when he learned that Honja could actually speak his language, but Honja had been hiding this fact from everyone.

Nobody ever thought to question how Honja could always understand them, despite portraying himself as being unable to speak.

Honja, being small and defenseless, was often frightened and insecure. Sadly, this led to his lack of courage to come out of his shell and interact with others. He had many fears, and the fear of rejection or being laughed at kept him from speaking. He was afraid of saying the wrong thing or making a mistake. His act kept him safe and at a distance from the others, which was the way he liked it.

Now, things had changed. Honja learned the importance of his friends, and the interdependency they all had on one another. He falsely believed that if he kept everyone at arm's length, he would not be wounded by any of them as easily.

Though Honja's logic made sense to him, he had deeply wounded and alienated Boaz. The others quickly forgave the little rabbit and moved on, but Boaz held a grudge. The lion kept thinking about how hard he worked to teach himself how to speak Honja's language and had often stood in as a translator or mediator between Honja and the others. So Honja's secret felt much more like a personal betrayal to Boaz.

Chingu observed how much Honja and the others changed since their adventure with White Cloud. They weren't as innocent as they had been before. They had been on many adventures since then, and each of them had grown into their new roles as a team.

Noah now had a beautiful metal staff to use in self-defense. He carried it on his back attached to a leather belt. Chingu had been spending a great deal of time teaching Noah how to use it properly. The lanky lion also carried a leather backpack over his staff weapon to carry other belongings.

Boaz had his own backpack and a belt with a money pouch. He was in charge of their finances and directions. He carried a number of maps, books, and navigational tools. He had been given a dagger for self-defense, but he often kept it stuffed in his pouch with everything else.

Caboose was outfitted in light armor that covered his entire body. It was designed in such a way that he could roll up into a ball and be protected from all sides. It made sense, considering that Caboose had a bad habit of wandering off into dangerous situations.

Honja was very small and virtually defenseless, so he was happy to get a piece of armor for his head. The helmet had a small, pointy horn at the end of his nose so he could head-butt enemies as a form of defense.

The cubs each cherished the unique and special items they had been given in exchange for their service to the anointed King of Leonne. Flurry and the others certainly had many stories to tell – if and when they ever got back home.

Flurry looked the same, with his blue scarf and side pouch. Drizzle still had his sword strapped to his side, but he now had a pair of boots, and he no longer wore his red scarf. He never explained to anyone why he had removed it. Secretly, Drizzle had purposed in his heart to never return to Ursus. He considered Chingu to be his family, now.

They had all changed a lot! Boaz had a lot more responsibility, Caboose paid better attention, Honja was more social, and Noah was well trained to defend them. Most importantly, Flurry had become more selfless and even treated Drizzle with kindness and friendship. Being together for so long in dangerous situations knit the group together in a way they had never been before.

Granted, Boaz still found Flurry to be infuriatingly annoying, but overall they each improved a lot.

The cubs were excited to be on their way back home, but travel took a lot longer in a region that was devoid of cars and airplanes for transportation. The nations with faster travel methods were well beyond the borders of animal kingdoms.

Traveling on foot was slow and tedious. Chingu had to take them on a route that was not a straight shot to Ursus, due to some regions being full of dangers that were too much for them to handle. As great of a warrior that Chingu was, he was not invulnerable, and he could not take on entire armies. Some territory was safer to circumnavigate. The Meowari from the land of Meowaritanga had a fearsome reputation, and were only one of several examples of places and things Chingu liked to avoid if possible.

The night drew late, and they all decided to get some shut-eye. They each lay in bed and waited for their much needed sleep to come upon them, which did not take long. However, Caboose could not sleep. He tossed and turned before he stated out loud, "I miss Mommy!"

The other cubs sat up from their beds. "I do, too, Caboose. I do, too," Boaz replied.

"*Nah doh!*" answered Honja.

Noah nodded his head as he looked to Flurry.

While he lay in bed, Flurry asked, "Guys, do you think Mommy is thinking about us?"

"I'd like to think so," came Boaz's reply.

"I mean, we've been gone for so long. What if she thinks that we're gone forever?" Flurry continued.

"What if she doesn't remember us?"

asked Caboose.

"Don't be silly," Flurry replied. "Of course she'll remember us." Then feeling a bit unsure of his statement, Flurry turned to Boaz for affirmation. "I mean, she'll totally remember us, right? Right, Boaz?"

"I'm sure she will," the lion cub replied. "What I wonder about is if she ever learned what happened to us, or if she's been wondering this whole time."

"If only I had that door thingy, then I could get us home," Flurry chimed back in.

"The what?" Boaz asked.

"You know! The door thingy that I use to get us places. It was under my bed."

"Maybe you should sleep with it from now on," came Drizzle's voice from across the room.

"Good idea!" Flurry exclaimed. "I'll be

sure to do that, when we get back." After a moment's pause, Flurry added with a hint of grief in his tone, "If ... we get back."

"Don't say that," was Boaz's concerned reply.

"Yeah!" Caboose chimed in.

"Just sayin'" answered Flurry.

"Guys! Let's just get some sleep! You can discuss it tomorrow," came Chingu's plea.

The cubs conversed a little longer, but eventually they all dozed off to sleep.

CHAPTER 2
HOMEWARD BOUND

The next day was a gloomy one. The clouds were thick and gray. The way they swirled reminded Caboose of something frothy, like one of his mother's yummy looking cappuccinos with its foamy, steamed milk.

There was a light sprinkling of rain coming down. Flurry looked out the window, pointed at the rain, and said, "Hey Drizzle, look! It's you!"

Flurry giggled to himself as Drizzle sarcastically replied, "Ha, ha, very funny."

"Where?" Caboose asked. He jumped up to the windowsill and looked out. "I don't see him," he added.

"Caboose, it's just a joke. He didn't mean it literally," Boaz replied.

"Oh," came Caboose's answer, though it was clear he had no idea what was going on.

The cubs all worked their way to the front door of the inn. Flurry opened it and stopped dead in his tracks. He could not believe who stood at the threshold. "Fall?" came his uncertain question.

"Flurry!" Fall shouted as she rushed in and hugged her brother. "I've missed you so much!"

Everyone in Flurry's company was dumbfounded. Flurry was especially perplexed. "How did you find us?" he asked.

"It wasn't easy, believe me!" came her

reply. "Vallidore and I have …"

"Doggy? He's here?" Flurry exclaimed with tremendous excitement in his voice.

"Yes, Flurry, but if you'd let me explain …"

Flurry rushed out the door and looked to and fro until he saw him. The large, white wolf stood in the street. Chingu, the Savannah cat, and Shinyuu stood near him. The wolf was magnificent to behold with the blue markings all over his fur and his piercing blue eyes.

"Doggy!" shouted Flurry as he ran up and hugged Vallidore's rain-soaked leg.

Vallidore let out a chuckle and replied, "Yes, I've missed you, too."

Flurry looked up at the giant wolf and asked, "How did you find us?"

"You know, I was trying to tell you that

already!" Fall shouted.

"Oh yeah, sorry about that." Flurry giggled with embarrassment.

"Mrs. Lee called Mr. Kringle when she couldn't find you."

"Who?"

"Mrs. Lee!"

"Who's that?" Flurry replied.

"What are you talking about?" exclaimed Fall. "You know, the one you call your mommy?"

"Her name is Mommy. I don't know who that other person is."

"Oh my word! I can't believe you're my brother!"

"Yeah, it's pretty awesome! I know," came Flurry's quick response.

Fall planted her face in her paws in unison with Noah, who shook his head with disbelief. Boaz chimed in, "Flurry, I don't think she meant that as a compliment."

"Sure she did!" Flurry answered and then turned back to pet Vallidore's damp leg. "So soft!" Flurry spoke to himself.

Fall shook her head, took in a deep breath, and began again. "Your 'mommy' called Mr. Kri …" Fall realized she was going to have a repeat of the previous conversation if she said 'Kringle', so she quickly corrected herself and continued. "I mean, your mommy called 'Santa' when she noticed you were missing."

"Oh no! Is she okay?" Flurry asked with a concerned tone.

"Yes, Flurry, she's fine. 'Santa' brought her to Ursus, and he sent out scouts to find you …"

"Boy scouts or girl scouts?" asked her

brother.

"It's a wonder we've survived this long, with him as our leader," muttered Boaz.

Fall continued. "It took about a week before he got word that you were at sea in a conflict with Black Bear'd. 'Santa' decided to send Vallidore out to get you, but I insisted on coming, too. Mama and Papa wouldn't let me, but I can be very persuasive. Not to mention that I wouldn't shut up until they agreed." Fall followed up her statement with a giggle.

"I'm here to bring all of you back," Vallidore interrupted.

"Yay!" shouted the cubs in unison. "We get to go home!"

"Wait! How long will that take?" Flurry asked hesitantly.

"Another two weeks, most likely,"

Vallidore answered.

The cubs all dropped their heads with disappointment at how long it would still be. They were ready for their road trip to be over.

"If it's all right with you, I'd like to tag along. I'm headed in that direction," said the Savannah cat.

"Oh! By the way," Flurry addressed his sister. "That's Purratus." Then he turned to the Savannah cat and added, "Purratus, that's my sister, Fall."

"It's an honor to meet you," answered the cat as he bowed to the young female cub.

"Yeah, we met him a couple of weeks ago. He's been with us ever since," Flurry remarked.

After the brief introductions, everyone prepared for their trip. The mayor of Monax, the town in which they had stayed for the night, came and offered five ymyu for Flurry and the others to ride.

Flurry observed how the ymyu's looked a lot like deer, but their heads resembled that of a rabbit. Little did Flurry know that they were renowned for their speed, but that did not matter. The only thing Flurry cared about was how cute they were.

"Hello, little ymyu, I'm Flurry!" said the cub as he petted one of them on the head. The ymyu were barely any bigger than Flurry himself.

Chingu and Shinyuu helped get the cubs bags attached to their respective ymyu and Purratus' gear paired with Vallidore.

Flurry noticed that Chingu, Shinyuu, and Drizzle seemed to be doing their own thing a few feet away. He quickly jumped down from his ymyu and rushed over to them.

Chingu and Shinyuu both stood next to Faith, with her reins in Chingu's paw. Drizzle joined them, climbed up on Faith, and they waved goodbye as they moved off in the opposite direction of Flurry and his group.

Flurry ran after them. "Wait a minute!" Flurry shouted. "Where are you going? We're going this way!" Flurry pointed in the other direction.

"They have a mission of their own," Vallidore spoke up. "There is something that Christopher wants Chingu to look into."

"They can't!" Flurry teared up. "We're a team!"

Chingu looked toward the ground. He knew Flurry would not understand. He had hoped to part ways quickly to avoid such an emotional goodbye. He, Shinyuu, and Drizzle had quietly informed the others, but did not know how to break the news to Flurry without eliciting the reaction they were now witnessing.

Flurry, still teary-eyed, then realized that Drizzle was with them, too.

"But, what about Drizzle?" Flurry asked. "The mission is for Chingu, not Drizzle." Flurry was in disbelief.

"I'm not going back," Drizzle replied.

"What?" Flurry exclaimed. "Why?" Flurry was shocked and stumbled backward as if he were about to fall down. Fall rushed over and put her arms around him.

"Ursus isn't my home anymore. It hasn't been for a long time before our adventure together even started. I've been traveling with Chingu for a while now. This began long before you and I met in Tigris. On the road with Chingu is where I belong."

Flurry could not believe what he heard. His tears freely flowed. Flurry freed himself from Fall's arms, rushed over to Drizzle, and gave him a prolonged hug. "I'm going to miss you."

"I'll miss you, too," Drizzle replied and wept along with Flurry.

Fall could not believe what she witnessed before her very eyes. Flurry and Drizzle used to despise each other. Fall cried, too. She wiped away her tears on the hem of her blue dress.

Caboose, Boaz, Noah, Honja, and Fall came over and gave Drizzle, Chingu, and Shinyuu goodbye hugs. Purratus shook paws with each of them. Vallidore bowed, and the red pandas, along with Drizzle, bowed in return.

Flurry and his gang got back up onto their ymyu's. Vallidore crouched down for Purratus to climb onto his back.

The white wolf stood back up, and strolled down the street. Flurry and his brothers looked back and waved to Drizzle as he and the red panda warriors went their own way.

Flurry wondered how long it would be before he ever saw Drizzle again. He continued to look over his shoulder until they disappeared over the horizon and out of sight.

Days passed. Vallidore led his caravan northwest, through the land of Erminea. The view was breathtakingly beautiful with the hues of yellow, orange, and red on all of the trees. They were also making great time.

The speed of the ymyu's and Vallidore allowed them to cover a lot more ground in a much shorter stretch of time. It had taken the better part of two months for Flurry and his crew to traverse the land of Leonne after they exited the territory of Panmeare. Their newest transportation was more than acceptable to them all. They were homesick and could not remember the last time they had seen their mother or father from Middleasia.

The days had blurred together for Flurry, his sister, and brothers. They had lost all sense of what day it was, and the only thing they seemed to care about was getting back home.

"So then I ran straight in, but there was this huge monster in the way. I knew they needed me, and I ..." Flurry relayed one of his stories to his sister.

Before he could finish, Vallidore came to a sudden halt, and Purratus raised his paw to indicate that everyone needed to keep silent. Purratus leapt down from the wolf and drew his weapons. In each paw, he held a crescent shaped blade. The unique looking sword was known as a khopesh.

"What is it?" Fall whispered to her brother.

"I'm pretty sure it means we are in danger," Flurry whispered back.

Fall had a worried look on her face as she glanced to and fro, but saw nothing but trees and vines.

Honja's ears perked up at the sound of a snapped twig. Honja had become invaluable to the group due to his exceptional hearing. The rabbit's ears twisted and turned in different directions as they honed in on the sounds.

Purratus looked to Honja, and the rabbit gave him a nod to indicate they were indeed in danger.

The cat looked at Noah and made a gesture they all knew was the run signal.

"Uhhh … this is where things get crazy," Flurry whispered to Fall.

More concerned than ever, Fall replied, "What does that mean?"

"Purratus told us that we are going to need to run when he tells us to."

"Run?" she gulped.

"Uh huh. Get ready."

Fall gripped the reins of her ymyu tightly. She began to panic. She had not been on an adventure since her visit to the ruined city of Agrio in the land of the Sourpie. Fall also recollected how that adventure did not go well for her.

"Meow!" shouted Purratus.

Flurry and the others raced off on their ymyu's. Noah led the group, while he held onto Honja tightly. Caboose, Boaz, Flurry, and Fall followed closely behind as they dashed through the wooded terrain.

Their ymyu's were so fast that Vallidore and Purratus were now far behind. The cubs seemed to be clear of danger when Flurry heard his sister scream.

"Whoa, boy!" Flurry called out to his ymyu as he pulled back on the reins. He turned and saw Fall on the ground. Her ymyu simply stood there beside her.

Flurry rushed back to his sister's aid and jumped down from his mount. "Are you okay?" he shouted. The ardor in his tone was apparent.

Fall sat in a patch of moss and rubbed her head. "Yeah, I just fell off that's all."

"Okay, well we need to get out of here. I'll help you back up," Flurry insisted nervously.

"I think I must've hit my head harder than I thought. Did you just offer to help me?" Fall replied.

"Not now, we have to get out of here!" answered her brother.

"Flurry! Hurry up!" Boaz shouted from up ahead.

Flurry looked up and saw the expression on their faces. Honja clearly heard the sounds of what seemed to be their pursuers. There came a wolf's howl off in the distance. Vallidore was in the heat of a battle.

Flurry quickly helped Fall back up to her ymyu and then rushed to mount his own. They were off, again, in the blink of an eye. Flurry rode hard to catch up with Noah in the lead.

Flurry addressed the lion. "I think we need to find a place to hide."

Noah nodded to show that he agreed.

"There!" Flurry pointed toward some ruins. The gang rode to the mouth of the stone megalith that stood alone in the autumn forest.

As the fuzzies hopped down from their ymyu's, Flurry and Boaz quickly grabbed some tree limbs and attempted to cover up their tracks by moving the dirt around with the leaves.

Noah stood guard with his metal staff while Caboose and Honja hid just inside the mouth of the entrance to a stone temple of some kind.

Flurry, Boaz, and Fall quickly ran to join the others and crouched down in the dark passageway.

"Oh no!" Boaz exclaimed. "We didn't hide the ymyu's."

"It's too late now. If we go back out there, they'll see us for sure. At least we have a chance to stay hidden if we remain inside," Flurry replied.

Fall looked at the carved markings on the walls and felt a bit of concern. "Uh, Flurry! Where are we?"

Flurry turned and saw the wall was covered with engravings that depicted danger for anyone that entered.

"Let's look around," said Caboose. He took one step in. A poisonous dart shot out of the mouth of a stone statue and hit him. "Ah!" Caboose shouted and leapt back.

The others were immediately concerned. Flurry rushed to Caboose's side, and Boaz investigated for a wound but found none. "Wow! You got really lucky!" Boaz informed the polar bear.

Noah walked over to where Caboose had been struck with the dart, leaned over, and picked it up. Flurry hurried over to examine it. "I don't think we're safe in here either. Uncle Chip warned me about places like this. There are all kinds of dangerous traps inside. I bet there is something amazing in here though. Maybe gold and other riches. Uncle Chip would love to see this place!" Flurry had such awe and wonder on his face as he visually appraised the statues, briefly forgetting the danger they were in.

"If Caboose hadn't been wearing armor, it would've likely killed him," Boaz inserted his opinion on the matter.

"I'll have to thank Yudel again for giving it to him," Flurry replied. Then with a determined look on his face, Flurry declared, "Okay, this place isn't safe either. Let's go to a different spot."

Flurry led the way, and they all raced across the leaf-covered ground to the adjacent structure. As they approached, Flurry could not help but notice that the statues seemed to resemble the golden statue that he had stashed away in his pouch from a previous adventure. Could this be the place he had been searching for since he left White Cloud's ship?

The cubs were near to their destination when their path was blocked. They all suddenly stopped in their tracks, which caused Caboose to crash into Fall.

Flurry had a bad feeling as one-by-one different cats dropped down from the trees above. They were surrounded. Their feline visitors appeared to all be female and were arrayed in attire that resembled the cats Flurry met in Tikalico. Each cat had a different color of fur with varied markings. They carried multiple weapons and appeared to be prepared to do battle.

The assassin cats encircled them. Flurry and his companions were filled with fear. The cats hissed and clawed at them. Without Vallidore or Purratus to protect them, they knew it would end badly for them.

CHAPTER 3
THE COST OF WAR

Flurry was quick-witted and was already devising an escape plan when one of the cats asked, "Which one of you is named Flurry?"

Nobody spoke up, but they unanimously glanced in Flurry's direction. "Thanks a lot, guys! Thanks a whole lot!" Flurry grumbled.

"You're Flurry?" the cat asked.

"I guess so, who's asking?" he replied.

"You don't get to ask questions. We're here to bring you to our queen. She's been waiting for this moment for a long time," answered the cat as she nodded to her comrades.

It was clear to Flurry that it was some kind of signal, and he did not think they were here to be friendly. Flurry glanced at the others and gave a nod of his own. The others indicated that they understood his subtle message.

Fall was the only one out of the loop. She did not realize that her brother had developed a code with the others for situations like this one. He indicated to the others that he was going to run, and they should try to escape.

Without a moment of hesitation, Flurry made his move. He tossed down his pouch and ran. Flurry was not being cowardly; he actually had a strategy to his retreat.

As Flurry ran, all but two of the cats

chased after him. Noah pulled out his staff and struck each of them. He and the other cubs made a run for it.

Noah and his followers sped through the woods as fast as they could go. Never once did any of them look over their shoulder to see if they were being pursued. If they had looked, their hearts would have melted to know that the two cat assassins were very close behind.

Noah and his friends did not get far before the cats cut them off and stood in their way, weapons drawn.

"That was a foolish move!" shouted one of the cats.

"No, it was their last move!" replied the other.

The two assassins hissed and raised their weapons to strike. Noah raised his staff in self-defense, but they knocked it from his paws. They postured for a final strike when a blood-curdling howl was heard. The assassins stopped and looked all about for the white wolf.

It was clear by their facial expressions that they feared the beast. "I don't see him, do you?" one of the assassins asked the other.

"No, but that doesn't mean he isn't here," came the reply.

"Be ready, you never know wh ..." the cat warrior stopped mid-sentence and fell to the ground.

The other feline turned and saw Purratus standing over her lifeless friend.

"Run! Vallidore will protect you!" Purratus shouted and pointed out their path of escape. The cubs dashed off and heard the sound of metal-on-metal from behind. They approached a white wolf running toward them.

"Where's Flurry?" Vallidore shouted.

Fall cried, "I don't know! He might be dead! The other cats chased after him!"

Vallidore growled. When he looked up, he saw Purratus draw near. "Stay here with them! I'm going after Flurry!" The white wolf ran off, and Purratus stood guard with his weapons ready.

Flurry ran as hard as he could, in order to reach the temple ahead of the assassins. He glanced back, but they were not there. Flurry assumed they were now hunting him and would remain hidden until they had their chance to get him.

"Well, I don't plan to make this easy for them," Flurry whispered to himself. He glanced down the long corridor of the temple. He knew full well that it was filled with lethal traps, but he had to trust his instincts and the knowledge passed down to him by his uncle in order to traverse such traps safely. He was relying on the temple itself to defend him.

Flurry pondered what would be the best route to take when the feline warriors entered the temple behind him.

"There he is! Get him!" shouted their leader.

Flurry did not have time to think anymore, he simply had to act. Flurry ran headlong into the temple, followed by his assailants.

The poisonous darts were the first obstacle. Flurry knew how they were set off because of Caboose's blunder. So he ran past them all, making sure not to trigger them. As the cats chased after him, a few of them were hit by poisonous darts before the others learned how to avoid them.

The assassins were cold and heartless. Not even the loss of their fallen companions slowed their pursuit.

Flurry did not know what had taken place behind him. He refused to look back, and remained focused on outpacing his attackers until he reached a large room with an open pit in the center. Flurry did not have time to wonder how deep the pit was; he simply climbed the wall in an attempt to reach the other side.

Luckily for Flurry, he was so light that he did not set off the trap. When the assassins caught up, the wall began to move as it reacted to their weight on the beams that protruded from the wall. Some beams extended while others retracted. This caused a few of the cats to fall into the pit, but others were fast enough to make it across.

By this point, Flurry reached the main chamber where he saw a pedestal with light shining down on a golden statue. *That looks like the one I have!* he briefly thought to himself. Flurry knew a trap would activate if the statue were to be removed. The cub picked up a stone from the floor and tossed it at the statue, knocking it from the pedestal.

At that moment, the entire room spun, segments of the floor lowered or rose, and the entire structure moved as if it were gears inside of a great clock.

The remaining assassins arrived and leapt from one gear-like platform to the next, in their devoted fervor to catch their quarry.

Flurry ran through the room and quickly ducked under the gears and slipped in between turning wheels. As if the stakes were not high enough, pillars came up from the ground and down from the ceiling. The stone shafts thrust up and down in an arbitrary fashion. It was utter chaos as Flurry tried to avoid being crushed.

He quickly ran across the room and back out the way he came in. The cats doubled back, but one-by-one they fell. Only two remained, and they chased the clever bear out the way he came in. Flurry rushed outside and over to where the ymyu's were tied.

Flurry panted heavily while he frantically tried to free one of the ymyu's, but he was too slow. The last two of the assassins rushed out and sprinted toward him. Flurry gasped at his impending doom. When the cub looked up and saw a great white beast standing on the stone temple behind them, he knew he would be all right.

Flurry felt relieved. "You should probably give up now," Flurry addressed the cats.

The two feline warriors stopped and drew their weapons before the leader asked, "And why is that?"

"Because I won," Flurry stated.

"Oh really? Is that so?" came a sarcastic reply.

"Yep!"

"Nonsense! There are two of us and only one of you!"

"Why don't you look behind you?" Flurry added.

"Do you think we're stupid? When we

look, you'll try to run," answered the cat. Just then Vallidore let out a howl and jumped down to the ground behind them. The wolf growled as he slowly approached the feline assassins.

The cats looked and saw the massive beast that towered over them with his teeth bared. He growled, and his blue eyes glared at the petite figures who now cowered in his presence. They quickly dropped their weapons and raised their paws in the air.

"We surrender!" exclaimed the leader of the last two assassins.

"Who said we were accepting prisoners?" Vallidore replied with an intimidating tone. His words evoked fear in the cats. They shook uncontrollably.

"Don't blame us! We were only following orders! We cannot disobey our queen," answered the subordinate of the two cats.

"Who is this queen you speak of?" asked the wolf.

"Her name is Necatual," answered the cat.

"Betrayer!" shouted the leader. She picked her weapon back up and leapt toward the other cat. The event happened so fast that Vallidore did not have time to intervene.

The first assassin fell to the ground lifeless. A brief moment later, her attacker swallowed something and collapsed beside her compatriot.

Flurry stood there with his jaw wide open. He had never seen something so horrible before.

"Turn your head, young one," Vallidore commanded, but Flurry was unable to look away. The cub was petrified.

As Flurry stood there in shock, many

footsteps approached from behind. "Flurry! Flurry! You're alive!" shouted his sister. Fall ran up and threw her arms around her brother. It took only a moment before she realized something was wrong. Flurry was not moving.

"Flurry? Flurry? Are you okay?" Fall asked as she waved her paw in front of his eyes.

Vallidore was concerned and turned to Purratus for help. "Please, take him to the steps. He needs some time to clear his head."

Purratus and Fall led Flurry away. Vallidore turned to Noah. "There is a river over there. Please get some water for Flurry and then return to fill up the rest of the flasks." Noah saluted, and ran off.

Vallidore turned his attention to Caboose,

Honja, and Boaz. The wolf commanded, "You three, please gather everyone's belongings and bring them to that clearing. It'll be dark soon. We'll camp here tonight."

The cubs ventured off to fulfill their duties. Purratus returned and helped Vallidore drag away the bodies of their would-be assassins.

"Did I hear you correctly?" asked Purratus. "We're making camp here?"

"Well, it's apparent that we're being hunted. Does it really matter where we camp? If there are others, they'll be coming no matter where we are. At least in this place we can take shelter inside and have stone walls to our backs," the wolf replied.

"I hope you're right," returned the Savannah cat.

The wolf looked at his new friend and

said, "Keep your eyes sharp. I think we're in for a long night."

The punctuality of the darkness was ever so reliable. It was one thing they could all count on for sure. Before long, the sky was the color of pitch, and Flurry remained seated in the same position for hours on end, unchanged. A frigid breeze rustled the canopy overhead while Fall perched by her brother's side.

Purratus approached with two bowls of soup freshly made by Boaz. Purratus handed one to each of the cubs, but only Fall responded. "Thank you," she replied as she took both of the bowls and set one next to her brother.

"How's he holding up?" asked Purratus.

"I don't know. I've never seen him like this. I hope he's okay," came the sibling's anguished response.

"It isn't common or appropriate for a little cub to see something so horrific. He's in shock," Purratus stated before he turned and walked away. The cat paused briefly, looked over his shoulder, and added, "Give him time."

Honja listened in from behind a broken stone slab that lay on the ground. Caboose just lay at Flurry's feet like loyal pup concerned for its master. Noah stood watch and tried to look brave, but he too was concerned for his friend. Even Boaz felt grieved, but did not want to show it. The lion focused on making dinner for everyone so he could avoid facing his feelings. None of them had seen Flurry so broken before, and it left them all disquieted.

Vallidore stood on the roof of a nearby

structure to keep watch. The wolf only took small nap breaks when Purratus stepped in and insisted.

"Flurry, everything will be okay. I want you to know that we all love you, and we're here for you if you need anything." Fall's words seemed to get carried off by the wind. Her brother remained frozen in place.

Fall picked up Flurry's bowl of soup, took a spoon full of it, and put it to his lips, but Flurry still would not respond. Tears slid down Fall's cheeks as she set the bowl back down beside her brother. "Flurry, you have to eat something. Flurry? Say something!"

After she realized Flurry was not going to eat, Fall ate her own bowl of soup. Tears trickled into her broth. Caboose stood up and laid his chin down on Flurry's leg. Flurry reached over to pet Caboose's head.

Fall looked up expectantly and wiped away her tears to observe. She was surprised that her brother responded to something. Then tears came down Flurry's cheeks. The cub mumbled something softly. Fall could not make out what he said.

"What?" Fall responded. "Could you say that again?"

Flurry languidly turned to look at his sister and delicately replied, "It's my fault ..." With sobs and sniffles breaking up his speech, he continued. "They're ... they're ... gone!" Flurry wept bitterly and buried his face in his paws.

The others rushed to his side, all but Vallidore. As they stood around him, Purratus kneeled down low and looked up the cub.

"It's not your fault. You were protecting

your friends and family. They attacked you, and you merely acted in self-defense. Nobody blames you," Purratus tried to ease the cub's pain.

"I wanted to help everyone. I never wanted this. I'm a bad bear! Mommy won't love me anymore if she finds out what I did!" Flurry lamented further.

"Flurry, you saved us. If not for your quick thinking, we would all be dead," Fall replied.

"Flurry, we're all alive thanks to you," Boaz spoke up.

Flurry looked up and wiped his tears away. "When we get back home, I'm never going to go on another adventure ever again. From now on, I'm going to be good, obey Mommy, and stay home."

Nobody knew how to reply, so Boaz

grabbed Flurry's bowl of soup and handed it to him. Flurry began to eat, and things seemed to be looking up.

The moon had finally ascended. The cubs tried to bolster Flurry's mood with jokes, songs, and impromptu skits. It helped a little bit; there were times where Flurry had a hint of a smile. Before long, their languor got the best of them, and they decided to call it a night.

Everyone took shelter in one of the abandoned structures and went to sleep. Vallidore and Purratus remained on guard.

"Well?" asked Purratus.

"I'm not sure," answered Vallidore. He gazed out toward the landscape. "My instinct tells me there's something there, but I don't see or hear anything."

Purratus looked in the same direction, but

could see nothing. Despite having the moonlight, the forest was exceptionally dark. The Savannah cat was about to shrug it off when his large ears turned in the direction of a strange sound. "Did you …?"

"Yes," answered Vallidore, indicating he had also heard the noise.

The cubs had been asleep for a few hours, but it was clear that they had overstayed their welcome. "Get the others. We're leaving," ordered the wolf.

Purratus jumped down from the roof and ran over to the shelter to wake the cubs. Vallidore followed close behind.

Purratus shook each of the drowsy little ones to rouse them from their slumber. "What is it? What's going on?" Boaz asked while fumbling for his glasses.

"Shhhhh!" answered Purratus. Then in a

whispered tone he added, "We're getting out of here. Let's try to do this as quietly as we can."

The cubs yawned and rubbed their eyes while they quickly gathered their belongings. Vallidore snapped his head around at the sound of something in the woods. He turned and ran out of the ruined masonry to investigate.

"Where's he going?" Caboose asked.

"It's okay, we'll be okay," Fall tried to comfort the little guy.

Flurry remained silent, but was active in making ready for a hasty retreat. Noah had his staff handy while Purratus kept his paws resting on each khopesh.

The cubs all ran toward their own ymyu and loaded up their bags. Honja did not have much to carry. He had his own little backpack and rode with Noah. He stood by while Noah prepared their ymyu. Honja abruptly came to attention.

"What is it? Do you hear somesing?" lisped Caboose.

The rabbit's ears twisted and turned to hone in on distant sounds. Honja nodded to indicate that there was indeed something there. Noah quickly put Honja into the lion's own backpack and mounted the ymyu. Purratus drew his khopeshes and continued to survey the area.

"What was that?" Fall called out with a shiver.

Flurry had been silent this entire time, but he too was aware of the sounds that now seemed to be all around them. Multiple footsteps and whispers were heard.

"Uh, guys …" Flurry finally spoke up.

"Exactly!" Boaz responded as he climbed up on his ymyu.

They were all about to ride off, when a dark and ominous creature stood in their path.

Fall screamed and Honja ducked back down inside Noah's backpack. It was a wolf, but it was not their friend Vallidore, who was now nowhere to be found.

The wolf was gray with darker gray markings all over its fur. Flurry was already devising a plan of escape. He assumed that was the only wolf they had to deal with, but he was wrong.

Twelve more wolves revealed themselves and surrounded their entire company. The canine entourage growled and snipped at the cubs. One of the wolves addressed Purratus. "Lay down your weapons, cat! We have you surrounded."

Purratus complied. The wolves growled and glared at him as if he was soon to be their next meal.

"You're coming with us. Luckily for you, we were ordered to bring all of you in alive … for now." The other wolves chuckled at his addendum.

The pack led their captives through the woods for what felt like hours to Flurry. The sun was already peeking over the horizon when they reached another set of ruins very similar to where they had camped prior.

These ruins were a bit more intact, and there was a palace beside a courtyard where the wolves escorted them. As Flurry looked around, he noticed some other prisoners. They reminded him of weasels, but their fur was pure white. They were clearly stricken with tremendous fear. Flurry could only imagine what the wolves were going to do with them, and he shuddered at the thought.

"Tie them up!" came a female voice. The wolves swiftly did as they were commanded.

"Hey! I know that voice!" shouted Fall.

"Me, too," Flurry replied.

The cubs looked over and saw another gray wolf with light blue markings on her fur and an earring in each ear. It was none other than Wolfhroc.

"What are you doing here?" Fall asked, while being forcibly tied to a piece of broken stone slab.

"I could ask you the same thing," Wolfhroc replied.

"We're heading home," Flurry interjected.

"Indeed you were, but you're crossing our territory." Then in a mocking tone, she added, "What? Didn't you know?" The lady wolf chuckled at herself.

Before Flurry could answer, a deep, resounding voice called out, "You mean they're crossing into MY territory!"

Flurry, Fall, and Caboose all gasped at the sight of Isangrim as he approached from behind his lady wolf.

"Yes, husband, of course," she answered and bowed. A hint of fear could be deduced from her tone. She bowed lower when he came close. He had dark gray fur, light markings on his upper legs, and metal plates of armor which sat upon his head. He was the most fearsome-looking of all the wolves, especially at this moment with red stains around his mouth from whatever he had been eating. From the fragments of white fur around his mouth, Flurry easily deduced where Isangrim's meal had originated.

"Uh oh," Flurry muttered under his breath. The cub then realized that it was not only the ermines that had white fur. A sinking feeling came over the cub as he prayed and hoped it was not Vallidore that Isangrim was feasting on. After all, nobody had seen the white wolf for a long while.

"Well now, if it isn't the one that deprived me of my victory over the Sourpie. I should gut you right here," Isangrim snarled. "But that would be too quick. I want something more painful for you."

Flurry winced at the statement and closed his eyes when Isangrim's red, stained snout was but a few inches from the cub's nose. The wolf peered at Flurry. Isangrim's brow twitched under the pressure of trying to contain his rage.

"You know, you sure could use a breath mint," Flurry unwisely pointed out.

Isangrim was taken aback at such audacity and was not sure what to say. After a brief pause he replied, "You're pretty bold, little one! Maybe I should remove your tongue first? What do you think?" Flurry tried to keep his eyes closed, but peeked. He saw the angry wolf's gaze beam back at him. "Mark my words, cub! We have unfinished business that I intend to rectify very soon!" Isangrim snipped at Flurry's face, as if he were going to bite him.

The evil wolf then turned to Fall. "I remember you, too. You're not as innocent as you'd have me believe. You fooled me once, but that won't happen again."

Last of all, he turned to face Caboose and remarked, "If it isn't the infamous wolf from the Turnip pack. What was your name again? Oh yes! Wolfy McWolfington, if my memory serves me well." Then with a smirk Isangrim added a sarcastic remark. "A really well thought-out name, I might add."

"Sank you!" Caboose replied.

Before Isangrim could respond, Flurry chimed in. "Well, you fell for it," he muttered under his breath.

"What was that?" Isangrim exclaimed. "If you have something to say, speak up!" Flurry kept silent. The wolf huffed with amusement at the sheer terror that had seized his captives. "I didn't think so!" Isangrim added.

Isangrim turned back toward Flurry and continued. "And who might these others be?

Your friends?" Isangrim laughed a horrible, crooked laugh. "No matter, you'll watch them all die, and then I'll finish up with you."

Isangrim looked at his wife and ordered, "You! See to it that none of them escape! If they do, you'll suffer my wrath!"

"Yes, master," answered Wolfhroc.

Isangrim addressed the other wolves that stood by. "You three! Go and fetch Necatual. Tell her we have her prize."

"Yes, your majesty," the wolves responded and ran off.

"I'll be back. I was in the middle of my morning meal." Flurry was pleased when he saw Isangrim walk off. He was more terrifying than Flurry remembered.

This is bad, this is really bad, Flurry thought to himself. *Think, Flurry, think.*

How are we going to get out of this mess? Flurry pondered their predicament long and hard. He had to devise a plan under Wolfhroc's nose, while she sat only a few yards away and watched them intently.

Flurry looked about and then noticed that Honja was missing. The wolves had tied everyone up but him. *Where could he be?* Flurry pondered. Then Flurry saw the little rabbit peek out of Noah's bag.

Flurry was on the verge of an idea, but he had to test the waters first. He glanced back at Wolfhroc to see if she had noticed his little friend or not. *I wonder how good her hearing is.* Flurry thought. *Maybe I can whisper to Fall.* "Fall!" Flurry whispered. "Fall! We need to come up with a plan."

"You know I can hear you, right?" Wolfhroc interjected.

Flurry giggled uneasily and grinned at the she wolf, in an attempt to pass off as innocent. Wolfhroc sighed and rolled her eyes at such a naïve play on Flurry's part.

"Why are you doing this?" Fall asked. "You helped us before. I can't believe you are as bad as you pretend to be."

"You know nothing of what you speak, fool!" Wolfhroc stood up and approached Fall. "Don't pretend to know me. You don't know me!"

"I can't believe you're so bad. I think you're just afraid of him!"

Fall's bold words were met with fierce anger. The wolf snipped at Fall, which caused the bear cub to shriek and jerk her head away. Flurry was enraged that Wolfhroc would threaten his sister. "Leave her alone, you … you meanie!"

"Well now! Aren't you the brave one?" Wolfhroc smirked as she turned away to resume her guard position. "No matter, you'll all be dead soon enough."

"Sooner than you think!" shouted another female voice. At least a dozen more wolves came into the camp, including the three Isangrim sent out. Riding on their backs were more cats that resembled the assassins who tried to kill them the day before.

"It's about time! Where have you been?" Wolfhroc replied.

"Seeing to personal matters. It turns out that the contingent I sent after them has been killed," replied the cat. Their feline leader had shiny golden fur and glimmering green eyes. She wore a headpiece with feathers, and it was clear she liked the color of purple; it was the most prominent hue among her vibrant garb. She had two bladed weapons that were reminiscent of sickles.

Necatual jumped down from the back of her wolf and marched over to the prisoners. "Which one of them is the one they call Flurry?"

Flurry's gang decided to try and do a better job of not revealing who he was this time, but Caboose quickly said, "He is!"

"Caboose!" they all disapprovingly shouted in unison.

"What?" he replied, unaware that he was not supposed to answer the enemy.

Flurry sighed and shook his head as Necatual approached. "Him? This is the hero of Agrio? Not a chance! I was expecting someone more formidable than … this! He's the one that defeated Isangrim?" Necatual could not contain her laughter. "I had no idea the mighty Isangrim could be defeated so easily! Ha, ha, ha, ha, ha!"

Wolfhroc growled at the cat. Necatual stowed the smile from her face and cleared her throat in response to the wolf's threat.

"Don't let his looks fool you; he's very crafty," Wolfhroc replied. "If you want something to laugh about, just know he also defeated Jack Frost and your father, to name a few. Are they also as laughable as you think Isangrim is?"

The tone became sober and the atmosphere was nearly palpable, but it was quickly broken by Flurry's sly comment. "Yeah, I am pretty awesome," the cub smugly added.

"Silence! You don't speak unless spoken to," Necatual shouted. "No matter! I'll have you …" Necatual paused when she saw

Purratus among the prisoners. She could not believe her eyes. It was as if everything else no longer mattered. She approached the Savannah cat, pulled out her blade, and lifted his chin.

Necatual gazed at Purratus' downtrodden face. "Well, well, well, if it isn't the infamous Purratus himself," she began. "As prepared as your reputation states, you sure seem to be in a bit of trouble." Necatual followed up her statement with a laugh. "Let me guess. You're on a mission to find me, aren't you?"

Purratus glared back at her, but did not answer. His silence angered her. She struck him across the face. "Speak to me when I address you! I am your queen!"

"No, you aren't! I'll never bow to you!" Purratus replied.

"You will bow to me! You will bow, even if it's the last thing you do before you die!"

"You're gravely mistaken. The Pharaoh will see to it that you're dealt with."

"My assassins are more than a match for his medjay," she scoffed.

"Really? I easily took out your entire company of assassins single-pawed."

Purratus' words infuriated Necatual further. She proceeded to beat Purratus, but her punishment was cut short by a howl.

Everyone looked up and beheld Vallidore. He stood high above them all. Necatual and Wolfhroc gazed at the white wolf with intense terror in their eyes. "You never told me they were in league with him!" Necatual shouted at Wolfhroc.

"I had no idea! This complicates things," Wolfhroc cried out in fear.

A few of the wolves bowed down before Vallidore. Wolfhroc quickly reprimanded them, "Stand up! Don't bow before that imposter! Isangrim is your jarl!"

"Indeed I am!" came Isangrim's voice. He stepped out from the palace ruins that he had previously been in, and gazed up at Vallidore. "I wondered when I'd see you again. I've been dying for a rematch."

"Then you shall have it, the rematch and dying!" snarled Vallidore as he leapt at Isangrim and tackled him to the ground.

Some of the wolves ran, Necatual hid, while others stood and watched their leader battle it out with the white wolf. This was Flurry's chance. While everyone was distracted, he knew he could make his escape. "Honja! Come quickly!" The little rabbit looked out and shook his head in fear.

"Please! We need you!"

Reluctantly, Honja climbed out of Noah's bag, ran to Flurry, and cut his ropes with the little horn at the nose of his head plate. Before long, Flurry was freed. The cub rushed to loose his friends' ropes.

"Honja, go free the weasels!" Honja nodded and rushed over to cut the ropes of Isangrim's other captives.

"Hurry, young one. Untie me so I can join the battle," Purratus insisted.

"No, we need to escape. If you rush in, you'll be captured again or worse," Flurry replied.

"We need to help!" Purratus insisted. He grabbed his blades and was about to join the fray.

"No, we need to run!" Flurry insisted.

"I don't care what you say. You aren't in

charge of me," Purratus added.

"Fine!" Flurry sighed and continued. "We'll do it your way. You can go fight them …" The bear paused for a moment, picked up Purratus' bag, and added, "If you want your bag, you have to catch me first!"

Flurry darted off followed by his friends and the ermine prisoners. Purratus and the others all ran off into the woods unnoticed.

Meanwhile, Vallidore and Isangrim raged on in battle. The wolves that had not run off stood by and watched them fight. The two warriors bit and struck each other repeatedly. It was unclear who would come out on top.

Isangrim clawed at the white wolf. He swung at him with his left paw and then his right. Vallidore ducked under both of Isangrim's swings and rammed his head into the villain's belly before he flipped Isangrim over his back.

Isangrim hit the ground hard. Vallidore turned and grabbed Isangrim by the throat. The evil wolf whimpered and cowered before the white wolf.

"No!" shouted Wolfhroc.

Vallidore lifted Isangrim up and threw him to the side. Their leader had been defeated and laid there heavily wounded. Wolfhroc rushed to his side and sobbed.

Vallidore turned to the wolves and addressed them. "Isangrim has been defeated. I'm your jarl now."

Some of the wolves bowed, while others grumbled and snickered. "Isangrim's our jarl, not you!" shouted one of the wolves.

"The law of Canidore states …" Vallidore began.

"We don't care about the law!" shouted another wolf.

"Nor Canidore!" bellowed a third.

"We've outgrown such an outdated society," came yet another opinion from the pack.

Isangrim's pack got riled up and were about to attack Vallidore, despite the law of Canidore which forbade such an uprising. Isangrim chuckled. "You see, they'll never be yours again. I'm their rightful jarl, not you! Besides, if you really want to quote the law to them, need I remind you that it expressly states that any wolf that commits treason can never be brought back into the fold, but shall be put to death? Either way you look at it, you lose!"

Some of the wolves appeared conflicted, while others wanted to rip Vallidore apart.

Isangrim propped himself up with one paw and looked at his loyal subjects and gave the command, "Attack!"

CHAPTER 4
COUNSEL OF KINGS

At Isangrim's command, some of the wolves turned on Vallidore with ferocious fervor. The divided pack charged the white wolf, but the pack's resolve was not unanimous. Some of the wolves rushed in and chose to defend Vallidore from the others.

"Go! Go now!" shouted one of the wolves. Vallidore was moved by such a sacrifice. He bowed before retreating into the woods.

Yelps could be heard from the brave

wolves that chose to defend Vallidore. Isangrim's pack ripped into them, and their pain could be heard as it echoed among the timber. Vallidore vanished through the distant foliage, but two wolves decided to pursue him amidst the infighting of the others.

Isangrim was without the strength to intervene in the chaos. Vallidore had dealt a major blow to Isangrim, and it would take weeks to heal from his injuries.

"Husband, I'm here. Let me help you," Wolfhroc made her request and attempted to get Isangrim to safety.

"Bring her to me," Isangrim mumbled under his breath.

"Who?" Wolfhroc replied.

"Necatual! Bring her to me!" Isangrim coughed and hacked.

"Try not to speak. You have some broken ribs. I'll be back shortly." Wolfhroc rushed off to fetch the self-proclaimed feline queen.

Meanwhile, Vallidore rushed through the woods, but it was immediately clear that he was being pursued. His predators howled as they attempted to chase him down.

Little did his pursuers know who they were dealing with. They were clearly younger wolves that had not known Vallidore when he was once the alpha wolf. Vallidore was more than a match for the two of them.

The white wolf decided he would use this to his advantage. He quickly changed his route and ventured down a different path. Isangrim's goons were none the wiser that they were headed into a trap.

Vallidore howled, and continued down

into a gorge lined with rocks on both sides. The wolves foolishly followed.

As Vallidore reached the base of the valley, he turned around to face the incoming opposition. A brook trickled over the rocks beside his massive, white paws.

Vallidore looked up and saw the two wolves that stood on rock outcroppings up above. They growled. One wolf leapt at Vallidore, followed closely by the other. The white wolf ducked under his first attacker, which caused the hasty wolf to slam into the rocks behind Vallidore. The second wolf tried to tackle Vallidore, but the white wolf was too strong. The fight was short, and Vallidore struck his attacker hard, planting him firmly into the ground.

The first wolf stood back up and shook himself off, but froze in place when he discerned that he was surrounded. Vallidore grinned and asked, "Is something wrong?"

All around the valley were Felonin cats with spears, knives, hatchets, bows, and arrows at the ready. Flurry skipped down the path toward Vallidore. "Look who we found!" Flurry exclaimed.

Fall trailed close behind and followed up his statement with, "Well, actually, they found us."

"I called for them last night, after you were captured," Vallidore stated. "In fact, I anticipated danger in this region and sent out a messenger long before Fall and I found you in Monax."

Flurry suddenly stopped dead in his tracks and said, "Oh!" Fall giggled at Flurry's surprised expression.

A black cat with a red cape and a large

headdress approached. "King Sourpuss!" Fall and Flurry exclaimed in unison.

"It's King Pan'twar, meow. I'm not known by 'Sourpuss' anymore," answered the black cat.

"Boy, are we glad to see you!" Flurry replied.

"Come! All of you! We must return to Tikalico. There we can discuss matters. It isn't far off."

"We're going back!" Fall excitedly shouted to Flurry and hugged him.

"Okay. Okay. That's enough," Flurry insisted as he tried to push his sister away.

Flurry, Vallidore, Purratus, and all of the others were escorted by the cat warriors from Tikalico. The feline conscripts bound the wolves and towed them along as prisoners of war.

After three entire days of travel, they had finally arrived in Tikalico. Flurry had been deeply concerned that more attacks would ensue, but the trip was quiet. *Have we finally rid ourselves of Isangrim?* Flurry wondered.

Upon their arrival in the beautiful, vibrantly-colored city, the cubs were treated to a spacious room filled with comfy pillows and tasty treats. Fall and Caboose spent a lot of their time jumping up and down on the bed. Honja and Boaz sat on opposite sides of the room. Boaz continued to glare at Honja while the rabbit tried to avoid eye contact. Noah and Flurry played a new game that Purratus taught them.

Noah finished moving his pawn along the checkered surface of the wooden box. Flurry tossed four strips of wood down and made his next move when his sister interrupted,

"Can you believe it?" Fall asked enthusiastically. "We're back in Tikalico! I never thought we'd see this place again."

"Yeah, it's pretty crazy," Flurry answered. "I'm just glad that we're somewhere I recognize. Finally! This means we aren't far from home."

"Yay!" Caboose replied.

Fall turned her attention to Boaz and continued. "You know, I'm sure your mommy's going to want to know why you and Honja won't talk to each other anymore."

"Who cares? It's none of her business, or yours!" snapped the angry little lion.

"Has anyone else noticed how moody Boaz has been lately?" Fall asked.

"Uh huh," answered Caboose.

"Yeah, he's been that way since the

beginning," Flurry replied.

"The beginning?" quizzed Fall.

"Yeah, he's always grumpy," answered her brother.

"No! I mean ..." Fall paused briefly. "What's going on between Boaz and Honja?"

"Oh, that!" Flurry replied. "Yeah, he's just mad that Honja can speak our language."

"He can?" Fall grinned and ran over to the little rabbit. "Hello, Honja!"

"Hello," came a timid reply from the brown bunny.

"Wait! You aren't mad?" Boaz inquired. His demeanor indicated that he was put off that Fall was not angry.

"No," came the young cub's reply. "Why would I be? Isn't that great? Now we can talk to him!"

"No! No! No!" shouted Boaz. "Don't you see? We always could talk to him! He just pretended that he couldn't speak!"

"I think you're being a bit harsh. Clearly, he's a shy little fellow," Fall answered.

Boaz was more irritated now that Fall defended his newfound enemy. He crossed his arms and turned his back on everyone with a huff.

Flurry added a sarcastic, "See! He's his usual self!"

Flurry giggled at his own comment. Then there was a knock at the door. Flurry looked up and saw that the door was already open, and King Ja'gwar stood at the threshold.

The king looked over at Boaz and then to Flurry and said, "That sounds strangely familiar. There's nothing more important than family. If my brother and I hadn't learned that lesson, our kingdom would still be divided to this day. I hope you learn this lesson before it's too late, young one." the king addressed Boaz with an authoritative and expectant gaze.

Boaz did not respond, but just sat there with his arms crossed.

After clearing his throat, the king turned toward Flurry and continued. "Anyway, I'm here for you."

"Me?" Flurry replied.

"Yes, you. Come with me, please," answered the king.

Flurry got up, grabbed his pouch, walked toward the door, and then turned back to Noah and said, "You better not cheat, while I'm away!"

Noah shook his head to indicate that

Flurry could trust him, but as soon as Flurry stepped out of the room, Noah moved some of his pieces forward and made a chuckling gesture.

Flurry walked down the long hallway with King Ja'gwar before he was led into a large room. It was a meeting place of some kind; benches lined the walls. It was open in the middle and had a podium so someone could stand in the center of the room. Flurry noticed that the ermines were seated on one of the benches.

"Wait here. Someone else will be here to escort you to the council chamber shortly," said one of the guards as they both walked out of the room with the king.

Flurry was uncertain what to do, so he nervously waved to the ermines and said, "Hey, guys!"

The ermines approached the young cub. "Thank you for saving us. We're eternally in your debt. If not for you, we would've been that thing's next meal," said the lead ermine.

"Oh, it was nothing," Flurry replied.

"Our nation is dwindling. Many of us have been killed by Isangrim and his wolves. Others have become bounty hunters or have joined militias to survive. Many of our kind have joined Jack Frost's army because of the promises he made to them."

"Jack? I thought he was dead!" Flurry exclaimed with a fear-riddled tone.

"No, he has a hidden base somewhere. He's been building a secret army for nearly eight months now," the ermine replied.

"This can't be! It just can't! I saw him die!"

"No, you saw him fall, but his body was

never found," came a new voice from behind.

Flurry turned and saw Purratus at the door. "When you and Chingu found me, I was in the custody of the Gatemakers, yes?"

"Uh huh," Flurry answered with a nod.

"I was hot on the trail of Jack Frost when he set a trap for me, and I fell right into it. If you hadn't come along, everything I know about his operation would've been lost. Thankfully, I arrived here safely. Sadly, I can't say the same for my compatriots."

"Your compa, what?"

"My fellow medjay. Pharaoh sent his best warriors to track down and kill Jack Frost. We never found him, and every one of my brothers in arms was brought down in an ambush."

"Oh no! That's terrible!" Flurry then

pondered Purratus' words and asked, "Wait! What kind of a bush?"

Purratus moved on, paying no heed to Flurry's question. "Apparently, Theran knew of our plans and sent a team of assassins. You've met them yourself, so you know what they're capable of."

"Uh huh," Flurry nodded his head vigorously.

"Necat is to blame. She frequently has some kind of dealings with Theran. I intend to exploit it to get to him. Through Theran, we can find Jack."

"Sounds like a plan." Flurry paused and then added, "Well, kind of. What's the plan, again?"

"That's why you're here. All of you, come with me."

After traversing a number of hallways and

corners, Purratus led Flurry and the ermine survivors to the council chamber. When they entered, Flurry saw a large, U-shaped table with many sitting around it. There appeared to be one of Necatual's assassins standing in the center opening. She had green eyes and black fur. To contrast the black was a white belly, chin, and toes.

"Someone get her! She's a one of the bad guys!" Flurry ran toward her. Nobody knew what Flurry thought he was going to do, but Purratus grabbed him as he tried to crawl under the table to get to her.

"Calm down, Flurry," King Pan'twar pleaded with the cub. "This is Ki'sa. She's with us."

"Who? What?" Flurry asked as Purratus drug him out from under the table. He was dumbfounded by Pan'twar's comment.

"Who is she? How did she? What? I'm so confused!"

Pan'twar motioned for Flurry to take a seat at the table. Purratus helped him get settled in and then took the seat at Flurry's right-hand side.

There were many at the table. In addition to King Pan'twar was his brother King Ja'gwar, Vallidore, Purratus, the ermine survivors, some of the Tikalico warriors, and a number of others that Flurry did not recognize.

King Ja'gwar stood up and addressed the room. "Greetings on behalf of my brother and me." Ja'gwar and Pan'twar both bowed. "We have called this assembly to discuss the next course of action."

Pan'twar spoke up. "As you all should know, Jack Frost is alive and well. He has been amassing great power in secret. We believe he's planning to strike Ursus and Polaris soon."

Ja'gwar continued. "His whereabouts are still unknown, but we believe we can intercept him when his army makes their first move."

The female cat, dressed as an assassin, joined in. "As some of you are aware, I was planted among Necatual's ranks to be a spy. She is very closely tied to Theran and takes orders from him. If we can capture her, we can get to Theran."

"Theran holds the key to finding out what Jack's plans are," Pan'twar continued. "It's a reasonable assumption that he still wants to destroy Ursus, but he's being craftier this time. His previous attack, nearly eight months ago, was hasty and ill-conceived."

"Meow, we're having trouble tracking him down," Ja'gwar spoke up. "The stoat community has been instrumental in our efforts. They have been the eyes and ears of the Protectors and have updated us frequently. Jack's next move is imminent."

"Imma what?" Flurry whispered to Purratus.

"He's attacking soon," Purratus replied to the cub.

"Oh no! I have to get back there and help them. My parents are there!" Flurry blurted out.

The room was silent for a moment before Vallidore spoke. "This council has been assembled to formulate a plan to prevent any harm from coming to anyone in Ursus or otherwise."

"An assembla … formu … Can you guys

use smaller words?" Flurry requested. A number of the members of the council chuckled.

Purratus stood up. "I think our next course of action is to set a trap for Necat and bring her in for questioning."

"I agree!" said one of the ermines.

"That's foolish, she'll never speak," remarked one of the cat guards.

"That may be true," Ki'sa replied. "She's strong-willed and has trained all of her subjects to seek death before giving up any information."

"I think I can get information out of her," claimed Pan'twar.

"How so?" asked Ja'gwar. It was clear that he did not expect his brother to have that sort of a response.

"She and I have a history. In fact, she's

the reason for the division of our kingdom. Necat has been seeking revenge for the death of her parents when Tikalico wiped out her city during the war. She blames you, Ja'gwar, and manipulated me into turning against you."

Gasps could be heard among the council. "The past is the past," Ja'gwar spoke up. He knew that he would need to hear more from his brother on that matter, but keeping the counsel on topic was of greater importance.

"That may be true, but she and I were romantically involved. I may be able to get her to divulge the information we need." Pan'twar concluded.

The council chatted amongst themselves for a while before Flurry's voice broke through. "Am I the only one that hasn't forgotten about Isangrim? They're partners!

What if he protects her?"

"Flurry has a valid point," Vallidore stated.

More deliberating took place before Ja'gwar addressed the room again. "Flurry may be correct. The best plan may be to not make a plan at all. We could escort everyone back home. It's likely they'll try to ambush the caravan." Ja'gwar then looked at Flurry and finished, "If you don't object, we'd like you to help us draw her in. She seems to be on a mission that involves you."

"What would it …" Flurry began.

Before Flurry could finish his sentence there was a shout from the door. "Don't do it!" came Fall's concerned voice.

"What?" murmured the crowd. "Who is this? How did she get in here?" came many whispers among the council members.

"They want to use you as bait, Flurry!"

"Fall, how did you find me?" Flurry replied.

"It wasn't hard. We can hear your voice a mile away," added the voice of Boaz.

Flurry saw all of his friends that stood at the door.

Vallidore spoke up. "It would seem that we left out some members of the council." With a glance at the kings Vallidore said, "Your highnesses, with your permission." The brothers nodded in approval. With a warm, inviting smile on his face, Vallidore motioned for the cubs to enter the chamber.

"We aren't letting them make you do anything without us. We're a team!" Fall stated firmly.

"Very well!" King Ja'gwar answered. "You may all be a part of our plan. Please listen carefully. This is what we have in mind."

Hours passed before Flurry and his gang exited the council chamber, followed by the ermines and the cat guards. One of the guards spoke some final words to Flurry before departing.

"Roger!" Flurry replied.

"Oh! Was that Roger?" Fall asked.

"Who?"

"The cat. Was that Roger?"

"No. I just wanted to use that word. I saw it in a movie. It means that I understand him," Flurry informed his sister.

With an extended sigh, Fall muttered to herself, "I should've known. Why do I even ask?"

Boaz witnessed the entire interaction and commented, "Are you sure you two are related?"

"Wow! Was that a joke?" Flurry quipped. "It's a miracle, everyone, Boaz made a joke!"

Fall and Flurry giggled, but Boaz looked annoyed, shook his head, and walked off. Honja watched as the little lion went his way. With his ears swooped back, Honja looked down at the ground and frowned.

"It's okay. He'll come around," Fall tried to encourage the rabbit without making the mistake of petting him. She recalled how much he hated to be petted.

The ermines said their goodbyes and walked away. Flurry realized that they might be the key to fulfilling his vow. "Guys! Wait!" the cub shouted and ran up to them. "I found this on a pirate ship." Flurry pulled the golden ermine from his pouch. "I think it might belong to you. I wanted to return it ever since I found it."

The ermines were speechless. Their leader held the statue in his paws and a tear came to his eye. "You have no idea what this means to us. This is a symbol of prosperity to our nation. With its return, it could restore our sense of purpose to Erminea. When this was lost, many of our kind lost hope in our future. Thank you so much! We're eternally indebted to you. If you need anything, anything at all, don't hesitate to ask."

Flurry felt good about himself as he watched the ermines walk away with his statue. Maybe he was making a difference after all.

CHAPTER 5
PURRATUS' FURY

The following day, preparations were being made for the capture of the infamous assassin, Necatual. Flurry stood by and watched as royal guards sharpened their blades and prepared their spears.

The Savannah cat worked all through the night to make sure everything was ready. He shouted orders while he paced to and fro in haste. The feline medjay checked and double-checked everything he could think of. He wanted to be prepared for anything.

Purratus seemed highly invested in their quest to capture Necatual. Flurry observed the Savannah cat for a bit before he inquired with the white wolf. "Doggy, why is Purratus so angry?"

"Necatual attempted to assassinate the Pharaoh of Savanis. She also killed Purratus' fellow medjay. So for him, it's personal. Both Purratus and Pan'twar have a personal stake in this venture," Vallidore replied.

"Ohhh," Flurry intoned. After a moment in thought he spoke up again. "Doggy, why didn't the other wolves follow you after you beat Isangrim? Isn't that what they were supposed to do?"

"Well, it's a little more complicated than that." Vallidore saw that Flurry gazed up at him expectantly. With a pleasant sigh, the white wolf agreed to explain it to the cub.

"You see, in Canidore …"

"What's that?"

"I was about to tell you," replied the wolf.

"Oh, sorry. Continue," Flurry added.

"In Canidore, where I come from, my kind holds very strictly to the law of the pack. Every new alpha male has the authority to forge new laws. No law can ever be changed or removed while that alpha lives. Only the new alpha can make changes to the law.

"When I became alpha of Pack Vallidore, before Isangrim usurped my right to rule, I upheld the laws from the previous alpha. The alpha that came before me was my father. His laws were good, and I saw no need to change any of his ways.

"One such law states that if a subordinate

wolf defeats the alpha in fair combat, then the new wolf becomes the alpha. My confrontation with Isangrim wasn't a fair fight. He set a trap and ambushed me, so he should have no rightful claim to rule. Nevertheless, in the eyes of my pack, he was their new alpha male.

"Because Isangrim is not the true alpha, the old laws still apply. The pack behaved treacherously. When I defeated Isangrim a few days ago, it was a fair fight. I should now be the alpha wolf, but the others refused to accept my restored title. Others ..." Vallidore paused briefly to collect his thoughts.

"Others? Others, what?" Flurry questioned. He had been intently invested in Vallidore's exposition.

"Some of the others showed signs of

wanting to join me, but I'm sure they are aware that if any wolf turns against their alpha, they cannot return to the alpha's service. It's treason, and the law states they shall be put to death.

"This has never happened before, but my nation takes the law of the pack seriously. By all intents and purposes, I've been restored as alpha, and they should all be put to death."

"Can't you change it? I mean, you're the alpha again," Flurry inquired.

"I was not fairly removed from my throne; it's been my rule all along, but Isangrim has been acting as alpha in my place. Technically all of my father's old laws still apply, and I cannot change them."

"Oh," came Flurry's sorrowful reply. "Maybe there's a way to work around it?"

"I'm afraid not," Vallidore answered.

"Okay, we're ready." Purratus announced.

"It's time!" Vallidore called out to everyone. "May the Great King guide and protect us this day."

The cat guards marched out of the city and across the bridge to the mainland.

At this time, Flurry's friends had arrived all prepared and ready to go. In no time, they were off along with the second wave of soldiers. The cubs rode upon their ymyu's close to Vallidore and Purratus as they crossed the bridge.

Purratus approached Vallidore to report. "Well, the spy has been sent back. Let's hope they haven't turned her or else they'll know our plan."

"I believe Ki'sa can be trusted," Vallidore replied.

"Are you sure this is safe?" Fall asked the feline medjay. "I mean, we just want to get home. We do not want to be thrown into a battle."

Before Purratus could answer, the wolf spoke up. "I agree! These young ones are but cubs. Christopher Kringle tasked me with getting them home safely. The only reason I even agreed to this plan is because the chances of the enemy attacking us on the way back home was already a certainty. It's better to be prepared than to be caught off guard."

Purratus reassured them that it was safe, and that they would make it home in one piece. "We've sent out a stealth team in advance to scout the area and keep watch well ahead of us. They'll make sure that nobody will be aware of our presence before we're aware of theirs. If they come across the enemy, their orders are to eliminate them."

"They're going to put plastic over them?" Flurry exclaimed. He was shocked, horrified, and confused.

"What?" Purratus asked, uncertain of what that even meant.

Fall and the others had dumbfounded looks on their faces.

"Oh my!" came Boaz's reply. "E-liminate … NOT laminate! I thought Drizzle taught you better than that!"

"What has Drizzle been teaching him?" Fall inquired. She was intrigued by what seemed implausible to her.

"He was supposed to be teaching Flurry how to read and was even trying to improve his vocabulary. It clearly hasn't stuck," Boaz answered.

Flurry simply sat upon his ymyu with an embarrassed grin on his face. "Not to change the subject, but we're no longer in the city. Okay, goodbye!" Flurry shouted out toward Tikalico. The other cubs turned back and waved, though there was nobody in particular they waved to.

There were two caravans that left Tikalico. After they exited the city, the caravans split into two groups. The first half of each group marched more quickly to create a gap between each company of troops. There were now four groups in total, with Flurry and his friends being in the third wave.

The trip was long, but familiar. Flurry and Fall looked around at the sights they had seen nearly a year ago. It looked a bit different, especially with the autumn leaves. Caboose should have recognized the area, but he was in his own world most of the time. Caboose lived a care-free life, not even realizing there were things that he should be concerned about. Sometimes, the others envied the little guy.

After a full day of travel, some words came that Flurry and the other cubs did not want to hear. "Make camp!" shouted one of the guards.

"Awww! Do we have to?" Flurry asked with great worriment to his tone. The last time they made camp they were ambushed. Flurry and the other cubs were frightened.

"It'll be all right, young ones. I'll never leave you, nor abandon you," Vallidore assured them. His words had a way of making anyone that was a friend feel safe.

As big and powerful as he was, he could either be a great ally, or a fearsome enemy.

Purratus had gone on ahead. He was anxious to be on the lookout for his quarry. He desperately wanted to haul Necatual back to Savanis to answer for her crimes.

The cubs huddled up close to each other for comfort and a sense of security. Boaz slept apart from the others. His attitude continued to sour with each passing day. The wound in his heart was quickly becoming gangrenous. If he could not bring himself to forgive Honja, the seed of bitterness would grow into hatred. Fall worried deeply for Boaz. She did not like what he was turning into. It was like the little lion she once knew was gone.

The cubs stared up at the stars. "Oooh! Look!" shouted Caboose.

"What? What was it?" Flurry inquired.

"One of suh diamonds fell," the plush polar bear responded.

"Diamonds?" Fall interjected with her bewildered tone.

"Yeah, he thinks that the stars are diamonds," Flurry replied. "He also thinks the moon is made out of cheese."

"Ohhh, I see." Fall then looked back at Caboose and asked, "Did you make a wish?"

"I don't know how to make sem. What are say made out of?"

Flurry chuckled. "No, silly! Wish for something!" Caboose giggled at Flurry's statement.

The polar bear thought about it and said, "I wish sat some of suh moon fell instead. Sen I can eat it."

Flurry bellowed loudly. That was the first

time he had experienced a good hearty laugh in so long. "Caboose! How many times have I told you? The moon isn't made out of cheese!"

"Yum! Yum!" came Caboose's response.

"Caboose! Make another wish," Fall added.

"I wish I was home whiss Mommy," lisped Caboose. "Does sat count?"

"*Na doh!*" came Honja's reply.

"What does that mean?" asked Fall.

Honja looked really timid and then softly responded, "Me, too."

"Awww! That's so cute!" If Fall had not been on the other side of her brother, she would have given Honja a great big hug just for being so adorable.

Flurry's countenance dropped. "Yeah, it doesn't seem like we'll ever make it home. I miss mommy, my bed, my stuffed bunny, hot chocolate, p'sghetti, and macamoni."

Fall bellowed further laughter. "What?" Flurry asked. He was confused by her sudden bout of the giggles. "What?" Flurry impatiently inquired again.

"Ha, ha, ha, ha, ha!" came more of his sister's liveliness. "You said macamoni instead of macaroni! Ha, ha, ha, ha, ha!"

"Whatever!" Flurry remarked, rolled over onto his side, and closed his eyes. His mood had quickly become sullen. He did not like to be laughed at, and Caboose reminded him of all the things he missed. A tear formed in his eye, so he tried to put it out of his mind and get some sleep.

Fall tried to stop laughing, but would have little spurts of giggles from time-to-time.

After a period of silence, Fall sat up to see if the rest of the cubs were still conscious or not. Noah waved to her, and she responded with, "Goodnight, Noah." She laid her head back down on her pillow, and then added, "Goodnight, everyone!"

Honja, Flurry, and Caboose replied softly, but Boaz ignored her. "Goodnight, Boaz! I love you!" There was no reply. Fall felt sad. She too wanted to get them all back home. Maybe then Boaz would be in a better state of mind.

The next morning came and went. They all found themselves on the road again. The group pushed north through forests, valleys, and meadows. Numerous times they came across hazards or dangerous wildlife, but the cubs were well-guarded by the Felonin warriors.

Their trip was uneventful for days. Flurry and the others hoped they might get all the way home without a skirmish of any kind. Their wishful thinking was not meant to be. After nearly a week of travel, they were met with disaster.

It all happened so suddenly. Flurry and the others ate lunch. A loud tumult was heard in the distance up ahead. Horns sounded. Their bellowing echoed through the wooded landscape.

Flurry rose to his feet before the others could react. The cub sprinted to one of the Felonin guards. "What's going on?"

"The first unit is under attack," came the guard's answer before running off.

"Doggy? Doggy? Where's Doggy?" Flurry's query made his dismay apparent.

"I'm right here, don't worry," came

Vallidore's reassuring tone. Flurry rushed over and clasped the wolf's leg with a death grip. "Easy there, my friend. I told you I'd protect you."

"Where's Purratus?" Fall nervously inquired.

"He has gone out ahead. He hopes to meet Necatual head on," the wolf remarked.

"What good is it if he gets himself killed?" she reckoned.

Vallidore was about to answer her when the bay of more horns was heard. "Quickly, on your mounts! We need to fall back. The first company has been overrun."

"This isn't good!" Flurry shouted. "Maybe we should hide!"

Vallidore considered Flurry's suggestion as a viable strategy if the second company were to also be defeated.

"Oh no! I hope Purratus is okay," Fall conveyed her deep concern. Her sights lingered on the battleground out ahead, hoping to catch a glimpse of their friend. After she mounted her ymyu, the cubs made their way back farther in the line.

Concurrently, Vallidore was in disbelief at what he witnessed. Smoke rose up from the fourth unit of Felonin troop's position. Nothing remained of their aft defenses. Peculiarly, not a single forewarning had been executed. Vallidore concluded that something had hit them hard and fast, curtailing them from even signaling for help.

Flurry and Vallidore traded concerned glances as they simultaneously reached the same realization: they had been flanked.

"We're surrounded!" Flurry shouted. He was not able to spot any enemies, but he was clever enough to know what was taking place. Flurry's quick-witted nature and swiftness on his feet was a true asset in situations like this. Before anyone else had a chance to digest what was happening, Flurry was already ruminating about what to do.

"Fall, Noah, Caboose, everybody! Off the ymyu's! We need to hide! Now!" Flurry commanded them like they were his own personal troops. They all alighted from their beasts and ran for cover among the bushes. Vallidore took cover behind an outcropping of boulders, ready to pounce any enemy that dared to come their way. The cat guards formed a perimeter with their swords and spears at the ready. Then they waited.

The sound of swords and battle cries hastily diminished. Now, nothing but large plumes of smoke rose up from the silent garrisons. Flurry and the others realized the frigid truth of their predicament. They were the last. Fall's chin quivered as she fought against the onslaught of tears that welled up behind her eyes. Hundreds of brave warriors had given their lives to protect her and the others. The reality of the horror was unthinkable.

Flurry and the other cubs continued to conceal themselves under brush and among the shrubbery. He could not fathom how a few cat assassins could have gained the upper hand on everyone. A revelation came when he heard bone-chilling howls. Necatual must still be teamed up with Isangrim's pack. They were not merely being attacked by Necatual's assassins; they were being hunted by wolves.

CHAPTER 6
THE STORM WOLF

Flurry scooted across the dirt on his belly to seek a better view. In the distance he could see the silhouettes of many figures that raced toward their location. A cold chill came over him as his fears were realized. It was Pack Isangrim.

Flurry could not keep still. He picked himself up from the turf, and ran over to Vallidore. "They're coming! I saw them! We need to get out of here!"

"Indeed!" answered the wolf. Vallidore

spoke with the guards that remained. They made arrangements to ensure that the cubs had a chance to escape to safety.

Vallidore crouched to allow all of the cubs to climb up on his back. "I'm telling you now, this won't be easy. I'm going to be running as hard as I can, so hang on tight!" the wolf instructed with an uneasy tone.

"No worries!" came Flurry's quick response. "I've got this!" The cub jogged up and climbed onto the wolf's back with a rope in his paw. "Here, everyone hold onto this."

The cats fastened the ropes around Vallidore's neck and then to each of the cubs. "Good luck!" declared the brave felines. "May the Great King guide all of you to safety!"

It grieved the wolf to ponder what these

brave souls from Tikalico were doing. "You'll be remembered for your sacrifice, and tales of your bravery will be told for generations to come. Thank you!" Vallidore responded.

"It is our honor and privilege to serve our kings. We will honor them in death, just as we have in life." The cats all bowed to the white wolf and turned to face the imminent entourage of ravenous wolves. A group of the cat warriors enacted their strategy to allow Vallidore and the cubs a fighting chance at survival.

The feline warriors were adequately skilled, but simply outnumbered. The troops took out three of Isangrim's subordinates quickly, which provided the opening Vallidore and the cubs needed. The white wolf launched through the chaotic skirmish and ran out across the meadow and down the hill. The cubs had a difficult time holding on as Vallidore raced to save their lives.

Their descent brought them into a ravine which, in turn, led them into another forested area. The ground was heavy-laden with leaves, and the trees were topped with orange and yellow. Here foliage was scarce, and stone boulders were plentiful. Ruins littered the area. Vallidore made his way for the megalithic structures. He had hoped that they would act as a ward when their predators arrived.

The wolf came to an abrupt halt and crouched down. "Hide! Quickly!" shouted the wolf.

Flurry and the other terrified cubs quickly disembarked and ran for cover under various slabs of fallen masonry. The sound of howls drew near. Vallidore paced between the decorative stonework. The ruins were once a beautiful feat of architecture, only to now be abandoned.

Vallidore was one of the world's mightiest and bravest of warriors. Compared to the other wolves, he was exceedingly larger and stronger. However, even such virtues could not save him from so many enemies. It was clear to him that Isangrim had gathered every wolf he could to join his cause. The outcome looked grim. Vallidore could only hope that at least the cubs would be spared.

Flurry watched as the wolves ran up to the towering stone walls and stopped. He was uncertain what kept them from entering. Instead, they just circled the area and growled as they peered in at Vallidore.

"My friends, you don't have to do this. I was once your jarl. Don't you remember?" Vallidore attempted to reason with them.

"You're wasting your breath, fool!" came a familiar voice. Flurry was certain it was the voice of Isangrim, but when he looked out from behind the stone slab he was horrified by what he saw.

Was that Isangrim? Flurry was not sure. With a strong, proud gait, a humongous wolf-like creature approached Vallidore. The beast had three tails, saber-like teeth, and large horns that rose up from each of his shoulders. The horns were each the length of one of the wolf's legs. Across the creature's body were flashes of red electricity. Isangrim's blood now coursed with lightning. His red eyes pulsed with bursts of pure, electrical energy.

"What in the …?" Vallidore murmured, under his breath, but his words were cut off.

"Are you pleased to see me, old friend?" Isangrim replied. "You might be thinking that I look better than I ever have. Well, you'd be right. I have Necatual to thank for this."

"You're not a wolf anymore. You're … you're an abomination!" came Vallidore's cutting accusation.

"Normally, a comment like that would've enraged me, but I've found a new collected me. I know full well that I'll kill you, and I take refuge in that."

"You may kill me, but you were never living, and now you've clearly traded your very soul!" Vallidore replied.

"My soul? Are you sure I ever had one?" Isangrim added. "I like my new form! It suits me, makes me stronger! I'm more than a match for you, now."

"I still don't understand. Why do any of the things you've done? There was no need for any of it. We were friends!" Flurry gasped at Vallidore's words. He could not even fathom how Vallidore could be friends with Isangrim.

Isangrim, in his newly acquired storm wolf form, chuckled with amusement. "I've done what I've done, because I can. I need no other reason."

Vallidore backed up slowly. Isangrim drew nearer. "If you wanted to lead, you could've been honest with me."

"Fool!" shouted the monster as he leapt at Vallidore. "It was about her! It has always been about her!"

"Kahneen?" Vallidore exclaimed with

surprise. "What does she have to do with any of this?"

"You've always had everything!" Isangrim yelled, and struck Vallidore across the face.

"No!" Flurry shouted. He was about to run out, but Fall grabbed him by the arm. A moment later, Wolfhroc stood over him and growled.

"What do you want done with this one, husband?" Wolfhroc inquired of her master.

"I'll make him watch as I kill his friends one-by-one, then I'll deal with him last of all. Keep watch over them, I'm not done with him, yet." Isangrim looked back at the wounded Vallidore and struck him again.

Vallidore chose not to defend himself. He knew it was a feeble effort against such odds. The other wolves watched. Flurry noticed that some of the wolves chuckled at Isangrim's display of strength while others flinched and looked away. One wolf looked particularly uneasy each time Isangrim struck Vallidore. Flurry pondered the situation and realized that this could be something he could exploit to create the advantage they needed.

"You! You!" Isangrim shouted. "It was always you! Your father was the alpha; it was only a matter of time before you took his place. That wasn't enough, was it? No! You had to have her, too! Her! Why do you get to have everything?"

Isangrim was clearly losing control over his emotions and continued to strike and beat down the white wolf with rage-filled attacks. Vallidore's blue, noble blood soaked his fur. Flurry and the other cubs wailed over the atrocious sight they beheld.

"Get up!" shouted the storm wolf. When Vallidore struggled to oblige, Isangrim shouted louder. "I said, get up!"

Vallidore attempted to rise to his feet, but his weakened legs wobbled from his lack of strength. He looked up and asked, "If you cared so much for Kahneen, where is she now?"

Vallidore's words enraged Isangrim further. The evil wolf clawed at and bit Vallidore, wounding him further.

"Fight, Doggy! Fight!" Flurry shouted between his sobs.

"Quiet!" came Wolfhroc's fierce warning, along with a snarl.

Flurry's face hardened. He turned to his sister and whispered, "Keep her distracted."

"Okay, but why?" Before Fall had

finished her sentence, Flurry was absent from sight. Fall turned her attention to the Isangrim's wife. "How can you not be upset that he's talking about another love? Aren't you even jealous?"

"I don't have to explain anything to you!" Wolfhroc snipped at Fall. "It's none of your business!"

"I don't know. It seems like he wants her more than you."

Falls words angered the she wolf further. "Watch your tongue, or I'll rip it out!"

Meanwhile, Flurry had slipped between the cracks in the stone just enough to get his head out. When he spotted one of the remorseful-looking wolves, Flurry went to work. "Hey! Hey! You, there!" The wolf seemed confused. "Yeah, you!"

The gray-furred canine approached.

"What is it you want?"

"I can tell you don't approve. Why don't you do anything?" Flurry asked. "You can't just let him die."

"I have no … 'we' have no choice," said the wolf. "We betrayed him long ago, we can never return to his service. Only in death can his law be overruled. Then, and only then, may a new alpha forgive our treason."

"So?" Flurry interjected. "Why not do the right thing, because it's the right thing?"

"That would certainly mean our deaths," the wolf replied.

"I see! You're a scaredy-cat!"

A bit angered, the wolf replied, "What did you just say?"

"I said you're a scaredy-cat!" Flurry saw that he might be getting through to the wolf. "Scaredy-cat! Scaredy-cat!"

"Hold your tongue, little one!" shouted the angered wolf.

"You're not a warrior. You're so afraid of dying that you'd just let a poor little cub, like me, die. Not much honor in that!"

The wolf leapt at Flurry. The cub quickly withdrew back through the crack in the stone. Before he could wriggle his way back out from where he entered, sharp teeth bit into his backside, drug him out, and tossed him to the ground. "That hurt!" shouted the cub.

"I should've known you were up to something!" Wolfhroc snarled.

Flurry peered at his sister expectantly. "Sorry! I tried to keep her distracted," Fall defended against her brother's downhearted expression.

"What did you do?" asked the she wolf.

"Nothing," came Flurry's reply.

Annoyed at his defiance, Wolfhroc decided to direct her inquiry to the wolves. "You there! What did this cub say?" The wolves acted as though they had no idea what she was talking about.

Wolfhroc let out a frustrated sigh and turned back toward Flurry. "I'm not letting you out of my sight! Don't you dare try anything else! I know how deceptive you can be!"

Flurry grinned nervously and stood there with his arms behind his back, like he often did when being scolded by his mother.

Flurry's words deeply penetrated the heart of the other wolf. He stood there and watched Isangrim continue to slowly kill Vallidore bit-by-bit. With each clawing, bite, or strike the wolf flinched and could not bear to watch. However, he found it hard to look away, too.

Another wolf approached him. "Well?"

"Well, what?" he replied.

"I overheard what the cub said to you. He has a point. We may not be able to be in our true jarl's service, but we can still do the right thing and honor him."

"Even if it means our death?"

"Yes, even if it means our death. We were all servants and protectors. How did we stoop so low as to join Isangrim? We made a mistake. This is a chance to right our wrongs."

"Then what is it you propose?"

Isangrim continued to scream and beat his opponent. Vallidore could barely move. His wounds were extensive. He looked out toward the rest of the pack, and a tear fell from his eye as he saw them just stand there and watch. His gaze brought further shame to the wolf that Flurry had spoken with.

Isangrim turned toward his subordinates and announced to everyone, "Behold! I am your true jarl! Let this day go down in history as the day I rightfully take my place as alpha over all of Canidore!" Without hesitation, Isangrim bit into Vallidore's throat, ending the white wolf's noble life in front of everyone.

"Noooooo!" Flurry screamed. Fall and the other cubs shrieked and cried when Isangrim threw Vallidore's lifeless body to the dirt.

Flurry tried to run out to Vallidore, but Wolfhroc blocked his path.

Isangrim stood proud with his crooked, evil grin on his face. His pack did not respond in a unified voice. Some of them cheered and mocked the lifeless wolf, while others were clearly dismayed. Before Isangrim had a chance to turn his attention to Flurry and the cubs, some of the wolves charged toward the storm wolf and attacked.

Other wolves followed suit and a skirmish broke out among the pack. Wolfhroc was torn between keeping an eye on the cubs, as she was told, and aiding her husband. Her affection got the better of her. She turned and dashed off to Isangrim's aid.

Flurry ran through the midst of the battle to reach his fallen friend. He did not care about the extreme danger he was in as he darted under the legs of the canine combatants.

Flurry reached Vallidore's empty husk, threw himself down before the wolf's neck, and bitterly wept. Flurry hugged the dead wolf and cried, "No, Doggy! No! Please don't be dead! You can't be dead! Don't do this! We need you! Doggy, please! I wish you were okay! Please don't be dead!"

Flurry cried profusely. It seemed as though his tears would never cease, but then something happened, something nobody expected. Flurry looked up and saw Vallidore draw breath again. The cub stood up, wiped his tears, and discovered that Vallidore's wounds had healed and his eyes opened.

"Doggy!" Flurry shouted and latched onto him for dear life. The cub hugged and hugged the wolf.

Isangrim continued to fight off his attackers, but in the midst of the fight he glimpsed Flurry at Vallidore's side. The storm wolf approached. "I try to keep my word, but I'm going to have to break it and kill you now." Isangrim grabbed Flurry with his razor-sharp teeth and threw him across the battlefield and into a wall. Isangrim chuckled to himself. "I think I'm going to enjoy this just as much as killing h..." He was interrupted mid-sentence when Vallidore leapt at him.

"Leave Flurry alone!" Vallidore shouted. The white wolf tackled Isangrim to the ground. Isangrim did not have a chance to catch his breath. Vallidore repeatedly struck him with all of his might. *This can't be happening. How can Vallidore be alive?* the villain questioned in his mind.

Isangrim struggled to regain some ground, but Vallidore's strength was more than he had ever witnessed in his foe before. Isangrim's attack against Flurry had enraged the white wolf. Vallidore was filled with adrenaline and anger. His blue markings and eyes glowed radiantly while he continued to beat Isangrim repeatedly.

The other wolves continued to battle each other. It was unclear which side would win until the sound of horns was heard. Flurry looked up and saw the Felonin cats, led by Purratus, charge into the ruins.

The feline warriors struck down many of Isangrim's devoted followers.

Purratus pulled his khopeshes free and swung them toward Wolfhroc. "You're not Necat, but you're in league with her."

The she wolf clawed at Purratus' face. His feline reflexes were quick and nimble. The wolf continued to swing and miss, while Purratus landed one strike after another.

The wounded Wolfhroc growled at her

enemy. "You were unable to defeat Necatual; what makes you think you can beat me?"

"I've already defeated you," the cat retorted. He had eyed a particular wall that looked like it would crash down with the most miniscule disturbance. He stood in front of it and waited.

Wolfhroc charged at Purratus, but the Savannah cat dodged the incoming wolf. Wolfhroc slammed into the stone wall. The megalithic slab rocked to and fro before it succumbed to its weakened integrity. Wolfhroc howled in terror as it collapsed on her.

Isangrim turned toward his spouse's shriek and beheld her pinned body beneath the massive stone. He felt helpless and unable to aid her. In fact, he was incapable of aiding himself. Isangrim suffered a ferocious bashing from the vehemently irate alpha wolf. Vallidore's love for Flurry and the other cubs fueled his strength and resolve to defeat his enemy.

Purratus approached Wolfhroc and added, "I may not have caught Necat this day, but I at least ended your evil ways." His blade swung low across her neck. Wolfhroc breathed her last breath.

"No!" shouted Isangrim. He would have run to her body, but Vallidore leapt at the storm wolf with full force. The white wolf grabbed one of Isangrim's leg spikes in his teeth, and snapped it in half. Isangrim wailed with pain. The once proud villain had been reduced to a whimpering dog as he tucked his tails and ran out of the camp.

The remaining wolves did not know what

to do. Isangrim had been defeated, Wolfhroc killed, and their leader had left them all behind to fend for themselves.

Those still loyal to Isangrim broke off their attack and retreated. The others that stood against the evil storm wolf remained. There were only twelve wolves that defended Vallidore and lived.

Vallidore's appearance was glorious. The true jarl and rightful alpha looked out over the wolves. They each bowed down before him. Vallidore's coat of fur was vibrant white, and his markings glowed a beautiful, glimmering blue. He looked stronger and even larger than before. There was no trace of his wounds.

One wolf spoke up. "We understand that we're deserving of death. Do with us as you wish."

Before Vallidore could speak, Flurry chimed in. "Actually, didn't you say that if your alpha died, you'd be free from the law?"

The wolf instantly looked up at Flurry and then back at Vallidore with an amazed expression on his face. All of the wolves appeared to have been taken aback. Vallidore smiled. "I believe he's correct. I did die. I cannot go against the law, and as the law states you are all now free from your crimes and may return to my service."

The wolves smiled and bowed before their new alpha. "I once again claim you as my own. You are now part of Pack Vallidore." Flurry, the cubs, Purratus, and the guards from Tikalico all cheered and the wolves howled. They had found victory that day, and Pack Vallidore had been restored.

However not everyone was pleased. Flurry looked and found Fall with Caboose. They sat near Wolfhroc's lifeless body. Flurry rushed over to his sister's side. "What's wrong?"

"Why did she have to die?" Fall asked while she wiped away tears.

"I don't understand," answered her brother. "She was one of the bad guys."

"Yes, but there was some good in her. I could see it."

Flurry did not know what to say. He flopped down between them both and put one arm around his sister and his other paw on Caboose's head to stroke the polar bear's fur. The three of them mourned her passing together.

CHAPTER 7
ON THE MOVE

The following day, they were all set to continue their trip home. Flurry and the other cubs said goodbye to the cats from Tikalico. They no longer needed the cats for protection now that they had Pack Vallidore to travel with them.

Purratus approached. "I guess this is goodbye. Flurry, thank you for all you did for me and for allowing me to be your travel companion."

"It was nothing," Flurry replied.

Purratus shook paws with the cub and bowed to the others.

"Where will you go?" Fall inquired of the warrior from Savanis.

"I have an assassin to catch and bring to Pharaoh for justice." Purratus turned to Vallidore. "I apologize for my folly. I was a fool to be so nearsighted. I was so blind with rage and my desire for revenge that I wasn't there for you when you needed me the most. I ordered the Felonin guards to pursue her. I was slow to realize that my place was to protect the cubs, but when I came to my senses I turned back. If I had been there, you might not have been killed."

"Think nothing of it. The past is in the past," replied the wolf.

"Speaking of which, how did that even happen?" Fall puzzled.

"Yeah! We didn't know you could do that," Boaz added.

"I didn't do it. I have no idea, what happened," answered the wolf. "I believe the Great King had his hand in this somehow."

Purratus bowed to the wolf and was joined by a small contingency of Felonin guards to aid him in hunting down Necatual and bringing her to justice. The rest of the troops marched back toward Tikalico.

The remaining trip to Ursus took another week. It would have been quicker, but Flurry insisted on helping others along their path as they worked their way back to the land of Mezarim.

When the wolves came across the mountains, the white wolf stopped to take in the view. The stars shone brightly, and the full moon had risen above their heads.

Flurry stood on the wolf's back. He looked back at his companions and said, "We're here!" The other cubs were half asleep on the backs of the other wolves, but Flurry's announcement livened them up in haste.

Flurry was relieved to finally be back. Filled with excitement, the cub looked out over the valley and pointed at Ursus. "Come on, Doggy! Let's go home!"

When they arrived, they were met with thunderous cheers. Flurry and Fall visually scoured the crowd for their parents. Upon their sighting, the siblings jumped down from their mount and ran into their mama and papa's arms.

Tears trickled down their faces as they hugged. Their embrace seemed to last for ages. It might have lasted longer if Flurry had not glimpsed someone he did not expect to see.

"Mommy?" Flurry let go of his papa and turned toward the young oriental lady. The cub cried harder and ran toward his adopted mother from Middleasia. The other cubs also bolted over to share in the love.

Flurry's mother could not hold back her tears of joy. It had been nearly three months since she had last seen any of her fuzzy boys.

"Mommy, we missed you!" declared Caboose. The other cubs agreed, in unison, while they continued to latch on to their mother.

The crowd of bears chuckled at the adorableness of it all. Vallidore approached a tall, muscular man in red. Christopher Kringle spoke in private with the wolf, while the other wolves stood and waited for their alpha's orders.

After some time conversing, Vallidore approached the cubs. "It was an honor to spend so much time with each of you. I'm glad you're all safe at last. Take care of each other," said the wolf as he bowed, turned, and walked away.

"Doggy, wait!" shouted Flurry. "You're leaving?"

"Yes, I am, young one. I have my kingdom to rule and citizens to protect," Vallidore replied.

"But ... but ..." Flurry sobbed. Tears flowed down the cubs cheeks. "When will I see you again?"

Vallidore smiled with compassion and empathy toward the young cub. The other cubs also cried at the news. They all came up and hugged the wolf's legs. Vallidore crouched down so they could hug him properly. The white wolf rubbed his furry face against each of the cubs and licked them on the cheek. "I love all of you very much. Be good to one another, always." The wolf glanced at Boaz and Honja when he spoke about being good to one another. Honja looked at Boaz. The lion turned his gaze to the ground.

Vallidore stood back up, but Flurry's grip around his neck was so tight that the cub dangled in the air from Vallidore's fur. Flurry's mother rushed up and plucked him from the wolf's neck. "Please don't go, Doggy! Please! Don't leave!" Flurry cried.

Vallidore signaled to his wolves to head out. As the wolves began their journey away from Ursus, Vallidore turned his head to look at Flurry, walked back up to the cub, and whispered in Flurry's ear, "Thank you for saving me."

Flurry suddenly stopped crying. He had no idea what that meant. He held a dumbfounded expression on his face while he pondered the meaning of those words. The cub glanced at Christopher Kringle for an explanation. Christopher smiled, but offered up no further details.

Flurry watched with teary eyes as the wolves departed. The cubs all waved goodbye. The wolves began their trek back to their homeland of Canidore. Flurry's mother held him until Vallidore and his pack were no longer in sight.

By this point, the other cubs had run off with Mr. and Mrs. Snow. There was a gathering at the Kringle home, and a meal was about to be served.

Flurry and his mother walked along the cobblestone path in the direction of the merriment. "Mommy, I'm sorry for making you mad at me."

"What do you mean, Sweetie?" she questioned.

"I mean, I feel bad for wanting to be a pirate," the cub continued.

"Flurry, that was months ago. It's water under the bridge."

"Oh ..."

"I would like to know why you neglected to tell me about that!" Flurry's mother pointed straight up at the centermost point in the northern sky. Directly above their heads was a beautiful sight unlike anything seen back in Middleasia.

Where Mrs. Lee expected to find Polaris, a red disc hovered above their heads with a bright light shining from behind it. Further above the first two lights was a giant golden disc with rings around it. Flurry's mother felt it almost looked like a red moon, a comet, and a ringed planet of some sort.

"Oh! Those? They've always been there. I never thought about it before. I just took it for granny I guess."

Flurry's mother laughed heartily. "You mean, granted, not granny."

"Yeah, that's what I said!" Flurry replied.

A great big smile came upon the young lady's face. Her boy was back and despite how much he had been through or seen, he would always be the same old Flurry she had grown to love more with each passing day. When she held Flurry in her arms, it was as if he had never left.

Flurry continued to give her his version of

an astronomy lesson. "The red one is named Gideon. The bright shiny one behind it is named Naava. The large one with rings is Kittim."

Flurry's mother was impressed that he knew the names of the nearby celestial bodies that stood overhead. She then thought to ask, "Does this world have a name?"

"Oh, Mommy! You're so silly! Of course it does! This is Ahelia," replied the cub. Flurry then paused. He recollected what Fall had told him back in Monax. The cub scratched his head and added, "Mommy, what's your name?"

The young woman was surprised by such a question. "It's Lynn. Didn't you already know that?"

"I thought it was Mommy."

Flurry's mother laughed and

affectionately hugged her little bear. "Oh, Flurry! You're so silly!"

"I love you, Mommy!"

"I love you, too!"

The night was extremely late, but there was a cause for great celebration. The cubs had returned safely and Isangrim had been defeated. Vallidore also survived, regained his pack, and once again became the rightful alpha of his land – not to mention that he finally was allowed to return to his home. After so many years, he was now Jarl Vallidore the Great.

The other bear cubs in Ursus were roused from their sleep so they could join in the fun. Christopher and his guest had sent them to bed hours ago, but they were not expecting Flurry's return so soon.

Flurry and Christopher hid away in the

study to have a heart-to-heart. "You know, I think the time has come that we talk about your situation."

Flurry was busy. He stuffed his face with the chocolate chip cookies Catherine had freshly baked. Only half listening, Flurry replied, "Uh huh," and continued to munch down on the tasty baked goods.

"You do know that you brought Vallidore back to life, don't you?"

Flurry stopped what he was doing, and wiped the chocolate from his mouth. "I didn't do that," replied the bear.

"Flurry, I've known about this for some time, but I've wrestled with whether I should tell you or not. I didn't know if you were mature enough to handle this information."

"I'm mature!" Flurry answered, took a

gulp of milk, and followed it up with a prolonged burp. Flurry looked over and saw Christopher gaze at him. The cub giggled nervously and said, "Just forget I did that."

The man laughed and then continued. "I don't know how this happened. The night I gave life to you, I discovered that you could already speak two languages, Polarin and English. I took note of it, since that has never happened before. Then there was the incident of the sun rising unexpectedly, and it has continued to do so on that same day every year. I spoke with the Great King, and he revealed that a part of the gift given to me has attached itself to you."

"Oh no! Does it bite? Get it off!" Flurry ran his paws all over his fur.

"No! It's not like that. Settle down. You have the ability to make your wishes come true."

"I do?" Flurry had a brief pause before he added, "I wish for a giant bowl of ice cream!" He sat up expectantly, but nothing happened.

"It doesn't work that way. It works when you wish for selfless things."

"I don't know what that means."

"When you wish for things that benefit others instead of yourself."

"Oh! I wish that Fall could have a giant bowl of ice cream!" Flurry jumped down from his chair and peeked out the door to see if she got it, but nothing happened.

"You see, this is why I didn't want to tell you. I was afraid you would abuse this power. Maybe I should request that the Great King take it away from you."

"No!" Flurry shouted. "I'll be good, I

promise!" The cub ran back to the chair, climbed up, and sat there looking more focused and serious. "If it's taken away, I won't be able to save Doggy."

Christopher smiled. "Good! The Great King himself monitors your wishes. Ultimately, he decides which ones he'll grant and which ones he won't. Use this power for good and don't abuse it."

"I promise to only use it for good," Flurry assured the jolly man that sat across from him.

The rest of the night was so wonderful that Flurry hoped it would last forever, but everyone realized they had been up the entire night and well into the early hours of the morning. The crowd had become sleepy, so they napped throughout most of the following day. Some of the bears went back to their homes, while other guests were given pillows and blankets to sleep in the large, cozy room together. The Kringle house was very large, and had many rooms. As Flurry frequently thought to himself – the Kringle house was like a castle.

When Flurry woke up, he noticed a young lady speaking with Catherine. The lady had long dark-brown hair and black stripes painted across her brown eyes. She appeared to be a Native American Indian. She wore black leather from head to toe, and did not seem to have a weapon of any kind. Flurry jumped out of his makeshift bed and ran up to her. "Hey! Don't I know you?"

The two women were surprised by the cub's intrusion, but the lady turned to him and said, "No, I don't believe we've met. My name is Nomika Ittindi, but you may call me Nomi. What's your name?"

Flurry paused for a moment and clutched his chin in thought. Then the cub's face lit up. "I know where I saw you! You were watching me when I was in the market at Tigris!"

"You've surely mistaken me for someone else," Nomi replied.

"Nope! I remember! You were watching us," the cub continued.

Just then there was a knock at the door. "Please excuse me," Catherine remarked to Nomi and the cub. The lady of the house opened the door, and a very tall predatory cat with a bushy mane was ushered into the house.

Flurry's jaw dropped open. He could not believe his eyes. He shouted, "Your majesty!" Before them all stood a regal-looking lion. He had two braids at each side of his face, shiny armor, a blue loin cloth, and a large sword and shield strapped to his back. Flurry and his friends ran up to the new guest and bowed before him.

"That isn't necessary. Please stand," intoned the lion as he motioned with his paw for the cubs to rise.

Flurry's mother was curious about the explanation of her cubs' behavior. "Flurry, what's going on?"

"That's King Yudel," Flurry enthusiastically replied.

"That may be so, but all of you ran up and bowed to him. Why?"

"Yeah, that's because we're his … what was the word for it?"

"Subjects!" Boaz finished.

"Yeah! That!" Flurry replied.

"Wait a minute, how did that happen?" Flurry's mother now wondered what other things Flurry had not told her. She knew she had a lot of catching up to do, since she had not seen her cubs in three months. However, she assumed that being a royal servant to a king would have been pretty high on Flurry's list of things to mention.

"We made a vow!" answered Caboose. Noah saluted her to indicate they were loyal soldiers. Their mother sighed and rubbed her eyes.

She cautiously approached the lion. Though he was a friend, he was a terrifying sight to see. His height was well over that of a human. Mrs. Lee nervously addressed the majestic figure. "Your majesty, I don't mean to be rude, but they're just children. Did you really need to enlist them?"

The regal warrior gave a warm smile. "Have no fear, I care very much for them," Yudel answered. He pulled the young lady aside and spoke quietly. "They helped me when I was in need. I gave each of them the honorary title of thane, and equipped them with defenses to ensure they arrived home safely. I would never expect them to go into battle for me or do anything dangerous. Have no fear; I care for them a great deal."

Catherine had not walked a few feet before there was another knock at the door. "This is a busy place tonight," she said as she answered the door yet again.

At the door stood three stoats with grave looks upon their faces. They each wore gray cloaks over their brown fur and white bellies. "We must speak with Mr. Kringle, it's urgent!" stated the leader of the bunch.

Catherine immediately rushed them to Christopher's study, introduced them to her husband, and shut them in.

"What was that all about?" Fall inquired.

"I don't know, but I intend to find out," Flurry replied, ran over to the door, and pressed his ear against it.

"Flurry! You know better! Get over here, right this instant!" Flurry's mother shouted.

"Yes, Mommy," came the cub's reluctant reply as he strolled back.

After a while, Christopher exited his study, thanked his visitors, and showed them out. The tall, bearded man then turned to his wife with a look of distress. "They bring dire news. The word is that Jack Frost survived his fall and has built an army in secret. Their contacts say that he's on the move. One of our lookouts failed to report in. The stoats sent out scouts and found that the polar bear army at Ursadoom has escaped. We have to move quickly! Gear up; I'm heading out as soon as everyone's ready."

Catherine nodded and rushed off. Flurry approached Christopher boldly. "If Jack's free, I'm coming with you!" Flurry insisted.

"Oh, no you aren't!" answered Flurry's human mother and teddy bear mother in unison.

Christopher turned to the cub, crouched down, and took the cub's paw in his hand. "I'm afraid not. Not this time. Do as your mothers say and stay out of this. It'll be safer for you and your friends if you do. I'll deal with Jack; he's my responsibility."

"But!" Flurry began.

"No, buts about it!" Christopher

answered.

"Are you at least going to bring Chingu? He's trained his whole life for this."

"Chingu is looking into another matter right now." Christopher stood back up and turned to the others in his home. After an apology for the sudden change in circumstances, he wished everyone well and left the room to prepare for battle.

Flurry looked to Yudel for support, but the lion shrugged. "I may be a king, but I'm not his king. He's free to do as he wishes."

"Flurry, get your things; we're going home. You'll be safe from Jack in Middleasia," Flurry's mother insisted.

Mr. and Mrs. Snow stood close by. When they heard the lady's idea, they quickly agreed. "Flurry, you and the others will be safe in their world. Take Fall with you, too."

"But what about you?" Flurry cried.

"We'll be fine, now do as she says. Pack your things and go stay with them." Mrs. Snow's eyes watered as she choked on her words. Fall and Flurry rushed over and hugged their mama and papa tightly.

"We don't want to go," Fall sobbed.

"Come with us!" Flurry added.

"We'll be fine, I promise!" Mrs. Snow attempted to console her cubs. Mr. Snow put a paw on the head of each of his cubs.

A bell rang outside. Flurry knew that signal well. It was implemented shortly after Jack had been freed from the ice. Flurry never dreamed that he'd witness its use. At that moment, Catherine returned dressed in pants and boots, with a quiver of arrows at her side, a dagger on her belt, and a bow in her hand.

"I'm gathering everyone here, so we can fortify the house. If we need to, we can escape through the secret passageways below the house. The elves have been summoned and are on their way." She glanced at Flurry and Fall, still clutching their teddy bear parents. "If you're leaving, you should do so now," Catherine explained as she handed Flurry the Ayever Del.

Flurry took the metal door handle from her hand, reluctantly, and stuffed it into his leather pouch.

Nomi approached Yudel and bowed before him. "Your majesty, I'm sorry that I wasn't able to speak with you sooner. I came bearing a parcel. I wanted to wait until you were alone, in case it is of a private nature."

Nomi reached into her leather pouch,

withdrew a rolled up piece of parchment, and handed it to the lion. Yudel focused his sight upon the wax seal that bore the sigil of Leomhann and was instantly intrigued.

Yudel bowed his head respectfully as Nomi placed the scroll in his outstretched paws. The noble lion broke the wax seal, unrolled the paper, and silently read the message. Flurry pretended to make preparations to leave with his family, but he kept a close eye on the situation. He was curious to know what was going on, and Flurry was not about to be kept out of the loop.

Yudel quickly rolled the letter back up and addressed the young lady. "Do you know what this says?"

"No, why?" Nomi replied.

Yudel looked to and fro. The house was

filled with activity, but nobody seemed to pay any attention to him or Nomi. Some of the guests were worried, while others conversed amongst themselves. Yudel turned toward Nomi, leaned close to her ear, and whispered, "Come with me."

The lion and the lady stepped outside. Flurry rushed over to the window and peeked out. The cub observed them walk a few yards away from the house and stop. Not to miss out on what the secret could be, Flurry snuck out of the house.

Flurry's family members and friends were busy gathering their belongings. None of the suspected that Flurry would run off at a time like this.

The cub hid behind a bush and listened in on the conversation. Yudel had a stern look upon his face, "The message came from a trusted source. They claim that Jack Frost is headed for the heart of Ahelia to obtain the Kaldur Stone."

Nomi's countenance dropped. "So he's not coming here? If that's true, he could turn our entire world into ice!"

"Indeed! This is grave news, for sure!"

"What shall we do?"

"We have to pursue him. Maybe we can make it to his destination first. We've got to stop him!"

"What about the rumors that his army's on the move? We can't take on an entire army! We should enlist Christopher's help."

"No! He has a mission of his own. If the polar bears have escaped Ursadoom, he will be needed there. If the polar bear army is with Jack, Christopher will make his way to us in time. We will be the first line of defense."

"We'd have to move quickly, if we are to stop this from happening."

"Indeed!" replied the lion. "Come!"

"Where are we going?" asked the lady.

"I have transportation for the two of us," Yudel answered as he briskly walked away. Nomi followed after the lion, and Flurry stealthily trailed behind them both.

Flurry could not believe what he had heard. If it was true, Christopher could either be led into a trap or on a false trail while the true threat would take everyone by surprise. Flurry did not know where Christopher was in the midst of the commotion and preparation for war. There was not time to warn anyone, and Flurry knew that if he reentered the house, his family would prevent him from doing what he was about to do.

Back inside the house, Flurry's family members were all ready to head to Middleasia. The cubs were packed up, but they noticed someone was absent.

"Guys, where's Flurry?" asked their mother.

"Uh, I don't know. I thought he was right here," Boaz answered.

"Flurry!" shouted Fall.

Mr. and Mrs. Snow helped to search all about the room, but found no sign of their son either. Concern laid hold. They were all afraid that Flurry may have done something rash – as he was known to do.

Christopher returned to the room. He was dressed for battle, with a magnificent sword strapped to his back. "I'm sorry to alarm all of you, but you really should head back," he addressed Mrs. Lee and the cubs.

Mr. Snow stepped forward. "Chris, Flurry is missing … again."

"What do you mean missing? He was just here," Christopher replied.

At that moment, the front door opened, and Flurry's cousin Bliz rushed in. He panted heavily as he tried to relay a message in between his gasps for air. "Flurry … Flurry …"

"Yes? What is it?" Mrs. Snow asked and rushed to Bliz's side.

"I saw him! He told me that he's going to stop Jack. He snuck into a bag on the back of a large lion creature that had horns on its head. Then a tall lion and a woman each got on one of those beasts, and they rode off together! I don't think they know that Flurry's there!"

Shock and disbelief came upon everyone. Christopher turned to Mrs. Lee. "You and your cubs should still continue as planned. Head back to Middleasia before things get worse. I will look for Flurry. He's likely headed to Ursadoom. I'll catch up with him along the way and send him home."

Meanwhile, Flurry remained hidden upon one of the two Leomhann beasts that served as Yudel and Nomi's transportation. As Flurry stowed away in one of their side pouches, he realized the consequences of his actions. The cub knew that he was about to embark on the most dangerous mission he had ever been on before.

Flurry wanted to protect his family and friends, so he had to do this on his own. If he involved the others, they could be harmed, and Flurry could not live with the knowledge of having put any of them at risk. Flurry hoped that they would be safe with Catherine or back in Middleasia. Flurry planned to save everyone and correct his mistake of freeing Jack eight months ago. Flurry would put an end to the evil Jack Frost, once and for all.

EPILOGUE
UNWELCOME VISITOR

The evening rays were well advanced and nearly extinguished. Necatual strolled down the back alley of a marketplace. The roads were still busy, but the merchants prepared to close up shop. The feline queen looked to and fro to ensure nobody had seen her make her way into the shadows. Before long, she was met by three of her fellow assassins. "What's the word on my father?" Necatual asked.

"He's very ill. The evil spirits that give

him his powers have taken a toll on him. He may not live for much longer like this," came the answer from her subordinate.

It was not the answer Necatual wanted to hear. A tear came to her eye. She hastily wiped it away. As the leader, she had to be strong. "I told him not to dabble in sorcery. He's so stubborn! It has led to his torment, and for what?"

The other cats shrugged. "Where is he meow?" Necatual asked.

"He's already on the move. Jack has enlisted his help to find the Kaldur Stone."

"I hope he'll be okay. I can't bear the thought of losing him, too."

"No need to worry about that. You have a more pressing matter to think about," came a new voice from the shadows.

Necatual and her assassins pulled out

their weapons and stood in a fighting stance, ready for battle. Out from the shadows strode Purratus. "I vowed to catch you, and meow I have!"

"Think again! I haven't been captured yet!" came the feline's snarky reply.

Purratus drew his blades and replied, "Put your weapons down; it's over!"

"Over my dead body!"

"That can be arranged." Purratus whistled, and a legion of cats from Tikalico revealed themselves. "We have you surrounded. There's nowhere to run!"

Necatual realized that she did not stand a chance, but her fiery spirit could not be squelched so easily. "You may have won today, but my father will come for me. When he does, you'll wish you had never laid a paw on me!"

Purratus stowed his weapons as the Tikalico warriors bound Necatual and her fellow assassins. Purratus smiled and drew near. "I don't think your father will be an issue. If what I hear is true, Theran may not live much longer."

ABOUT J.S. SKYE

J.S. Skye grew up in the Midwestern region of the United States. At a very young age, it was apparent that he was very talented. Finding that he was gifted in music and art, he plunged himself into both. As time passed, he set aside music to focus even more of his attention on developing his skills as an illustrator.

All throughout his years in school, J.S. Skye spent every available moment creating and developing fictional worlds. Caring about realism, he developed multiple people groups, countries, worlds, and even languages. His fictional realms were created through both written and visual mediums.

After traveling to almost a dozen different countries and studying different cultures, J.S. Skye decided to implement his interests in ancient cultures, history, languages, mythology, and more into his writings. He decided it was best to pour his heart and passion into writing instead of having divided interests between both art and literature.

J.S. Skye has accumulated a fairly large collection of his various writings. These stories range from all types of different genres such as mystery, science fiction, fantasy, and even horror. Friends encouraged the aspiring writer to produce a novel and see how things progressed from there.

J.S. Skye's first novel, *The Granted Wish*, was met with cheerful affirmation. The positive feedback was overwhelming and unexpected. Fans of his *Flurry the Bear* novels grew and began to clamor for more. From this point forward, his first novel series came to be.

For more information or to get in touch with J.S. Skye personally, he may be contacted by e-mail at:

JS-Skye@FlurryTheBear.com

ALSO BY J.S. SKYE

Flurry the Bear – The Granted Wish

Flurry the Bear – The Land of the Sourpie

Flurry the Bear – The Throne of Frost

Flurry the Bear – The Book of Snow

Flurry the Bear – The Rising Tide